YOUR SONS AND YOUR DAUGHTERS ARE BEYOND

ROSIE GARLAND

First published 19th January 2025 by Fly on the Wall Press
Published in the UK by
Fly on the Wall Press
56 High Lea Rd
New Mills
Derbyshire
SK22 3DP

www.flyonthewallpress.co.uk
ISBN: 978-1-915789-36-5
EBook: 978-1-915789-37-2
Copyright Rosie Garland © 2025

A CIP Catalogue record for this book is available from the British Library.

For Dad -
You were my dirty British coaster with a salt-caked
smoke stack

(John Masefield - Cargoes)

CONTENTS

YOUR SONS AND YOUR DAUGHTERS
ARE BEYOND

It happens when you're not looking. On Friday they are children, by the end of the weekend they are not. Journalists drive in from five counties and throng the school gates, arms in vertical salute as they snap picture after picture. You watch the news: kids covered head to foot with pelts of rough hair, bright orange eyes, mouths bristling with pointed teeth. Rather than shying away from the forest of microphones, they run circles around stupid questions. It's as though sprouting fur has given them power over words.

Under your roof, your daughter is first to change. You clap your son on the shoulder and say, "You and me against the world, boy". But his body is a half-inch to the left of where it should be; your hand slips its hold in a way that means he can't join in the necessary laughter. You raise your fist to have another run at it, but he's no longer in the room.

Details come in of an outbreak in Philadelphia. An elementary school in Adelaide. Reports from Khartoum, Brazzaville, Gothenburg, Edinburgh, Minsk, Kyoto. By the end of the week, you lose track.

You hear your son and daughter hissing to each other, behind doors you can't find the key for. Your wife says they're discussing online makeup tutorials. You ask how she can understand that garbage they speak, and the look she gives you prickles with so many sharp edges that you have to ask again, and again, until she's not in the room either, and you wonder what's going on in this damn house that no-one except you can stand in the same damn place for more than thirty seconds.

You watch your wife, studying her body for shadows where there should be light. Your questions used to make her agree with you, and quickly. Now, when you ask, she says she's stopped shaving her armpits, her legs. You laugh, and say, "What next?" You watch your son, but it's too late.

These kids make you want to vomit. Not the hair: that could be got rid of with a good fine pair of shears. What's needed are the good fine hands of buddies holding them down while you do just that.

You hate the way they aren't afraid. Kids ought to be afraid, ought to toe your line, no questions dared and flinching when you show them the back of your hand. You were promised fear and you want it back. You need it. What are you supposed to do, now that it's gone? Your wife says, "You could try…" but before she can add some raccoon-like word – *listening* for example – she's disappeared again.

Look at them. Their lack of self-disgust; their tails flicking in a tick-tock of *touch me and I'll take your hand off at the wrist*. How dare they be happy with themselves when they're revolting? You should be the one deciding what makes them happy and what doesn't. It's not normal. It's not right. They make you sick. Not a *Yes sir!* in the whole rat pack. Military service. Now, that would shake them up good and proper. Knock them into shape.

You're no-one's dog and you're not out of tricks, no sir. You check the house, day and night, but somehow, they contrive to be in the room behind you, or the one you have yet to enter. You try standing still, but so do they, in a game of musical statues to the tune of your breathing.

You keep the curtains closed. Outside, the world is roaring. You tell yourself it is the wind.

PRINCESS, STAR, BRILLIANT

He names us for what is most precious: Pearl, Ruby, Amber, Jade; and I am Emerald. A man such as Papa does not toy with vulgar flower names: those tedious bouquets of Lilies, Roses and Jasmines that delight at bloom's instant, but rot right after the taking. As Papa has it, a flower sickens after it is cut, whereas a gem grows ever more valuable.

I am the youngest. I am also the prettiest, though I will deny it in public, for lies are becoming. They bring husbands of gold and steel, in whom a girl may set herself to her best advantage.

Five daughters, blessed with a father who has never once complained at the lack of sons, nor rejected our mother for her womb's imperfection. Though we are female, he treats us as prized objects. He has assured us that if he were to sever his agreement with Mama, we would not be cast out with her. Are we not the most enviable of creatures? We breathe relief; gather ourselves into the safe shelter of his hands, and all is well.

Our days are filled with private study, and Papa is the sweetest of teachers. From him we learn our quality, and how it may be raised with the touch of a meticulous man. Does a jewel not beautify by being turned over and over in the hand of an expert? Papa takes each sister in turn to demonstrate the truth of it. He permits us to observe how he handles us, girl after girl, so that we may learn the necessary procedures we shall undergo. We practice new words: *connoisseur, sybarite, gratification.*

"Shhh," says Papa. "This is our secret."

Secrets are the most delectable of morsels. We sisters share them, luscious as caramels hoarded from the Feast of the Three Kings, although that comes but once a year, and our tutelage in pleasure comes so many times it is impolite to keep count. A lady does not keep count. If she counts, she is not worthy of that which is counted.

Papa may expend long moments on my sisters, but the longest, by far, are spent on me. I am his special girl, singled out for special schooling. He whispers, "You are the greatest of my achievements." What daughter would not give anything to hear those words spoken by her Papa? I learn quickly at his knee. Drink each drop of masculine wisdom; fatten on knowledge he reserves for me. Oh Papa, sun of my life, who teaches me how to be the best of gems: to glint, to shimmer, to draw the eye of discerning men. I dream of the ways I shall be cut: heart, marquise, princess, star, brilliant.

In all families, there is an occlusion in the stone. Another daughter is birthed, and this time Mama has done too much insult and we do not see her again. But what a pet we make of little sister! Blessed with the name Diamond: radiant eyes, radiant face and incandescent happiness. I am not jealous. Not a bit of it, for Papa strokes my hair and tells me how Emerald is a rare creature, whereas Diamonds, for all the money that can be made, are found in great quantity. Papa always knows how to soothe me.

However, even gods make mistakes. If there were ever an error in Papa's judgement, it is to leave the cutting of this youngest gem too late. She grows up strange. Answers only to Di, even when I hazard it is a sure way to bring misfortune onto a girl's head. She wears her hair and body in a careless fashion and when I say she is like a boy, she roars laughter and asks, "What is wrong with that?"

I clap my hands to my ears, chide her for her noise and clatter. I care for her, and wish her no harm, only for her to be less in love with ugliness. I try to instruct her about the many ways she can be made beautiful, tell her of princess, star, and brilliant.

"Half the stone is sacrificed when it's cut," she scoffs. "I'll stay rough, and keep every part intact."

"And never shine?" I sneer, displaying the smirk Papa has complimented me upon.

"There are better things in life than glittering to please another."

"It is better not to be, than be unworked."

"Who spouts that rubbish?"

I confess this makes me angry, for they are Papa's words, and no-one may slander Him. I will bear any manner of slight, but will countenance no-one who offends Our Father, even if she is His blood. Which one may doubt, for why else did he put Mama aside, unless she made filth with a stranger? It is what women do, those with a flawed womb. I toss my head; call her a fool, how she should kneel in gratitude that I deign to pass my secret knowledge on to her. I tell her of Papa's special love, exceeding any love she can hope to win. I rant and rail at her refusal to learn, her wilful ignorance of all that is important.

When I am finished, I wipe my chin of spittle and compose my hands into a tidy arrangement. I wait for her to weep and beg forgiveness, this disobedient beast who presumes to make me feel small. But instead, she speaks quietly. Such words as I can never repeat, nor soil my tongue. She twists his gifts into vileness, his special secrets into sickness. She tells me I must escape, before it is too late. I do not understand such madness, nor do I wish to.

Next morning there is a rope of knotted sheets hung from her window, a crushed rosebush at its foot. I pretend grief at the appointed times, when sorrow may be shown to its best advantage. Perhaps she is with Mama and all the other useless, unruly women. If it were not a misfortune of their own making, I might feel pity for them: the imprecision of their flesh; how their bodies spread like mongrel weeds; their lives of hideous work; the way they drag down the delicate reputation of our sex; that they have only each other, whereas I have everything a girl can dream of.

There is value in scarcity. We are five again and need no more sisters. Without her distraction, I shine brighter. I do not miss her. Yet, at night, her words hover around my head and whine like mosquitoes. One day, I will crush them and all memory of her. See, I have almost snuffed out her name.

One by one, my elder sisters go, to be clawset in fine marriages. I grow, and as my body blooms I rejoice in each of Papa's lessons. His hands, precise and steady as a cutter of gems. I strive to become perfect. I gleam. I glitter. He displays me, often. I turn slowly, to show off each pretty part. There are crowds of eyes upon every gleaming piece of me. Their gaze increases my beauty, and beauty is my value. What a price I will fetch! How I will crow when all is signed and done and I am given over to be hammered, clamped, burnished and secured in claws. Look deep, and in me you will not find the tiniest fault. I am princess, star, brilliant.

BURNING GIRL

She begins in a shower of crimson sparks. Sets the flame of her finger to the blue touchpaper of the umbilicus and *whoosh!* Out she flies, a rocket of a girl.

"Look mama!" she says, splashing the bathwater and raising puffs of steam. Her mother looks the other way, pretends she can't see silver chains of bubbles foam through baby fingers.

"Listen mama!" she says, giggling as her lips sizzle round the spoon when her mother feeds mashed carrot into the little cave of her mouth. Her mother is still looking the other way.

"Look mama!" she cries, running round the garden, scorching rings into the grass, streaming a comet's tail. Her mother buys gravel, drowns green under grey. Draws the curtains and keeps them closed. Hangs a fire-blanket in the kitchen, another in the bathroom, the bedroom, top and bottom of the stairs. Arranges buckets heaped with sand next to every door.

"Mama, you can't catch me!" she says. It's a hoot, a whoop, a loop-the-loop as she races up and down the supermarket aisles, her incandescence rattling the shelves. Her mother gives chase, flings a coat around her and hurls her to the ground while shoppers gawp and talk of ambulances. The hollow cluck of her mother's excuses: *it's ok. There's no need. She's fine.* And she is fine. She's a furnace child. Can't hold it in. Who would want to? She shrieks with laughter as her mother rolls her backwards, forwards till the flames wink out.

"It's time we had a talk," her mother says. They sit with knees kissing, hands locked in laps. She watches her mother's face press itself into serious creases. There's talk of danger; the need for silence; secrets. *Secrets?* The girl smiles, sticks out her thumb and up pops a hot petal from the tip, wavering from green to yellow. Her mother licks her fingers, squeezes it to nothing with a damp hiss.

"But mama," says the girl. "Don't you love the way I glow?"

"I'm afraid. For you." The pause between the words is less than a flicker of breath.

The girl laughs. "How silly! Who's afraid of a girl who shines bright?"

Her mother persists, warnings sharp enough to strike sparks. How the world hates what it doesn't understand; breaks what it hates. How she's only trying to protect her. On and on, in a cold and soaking voice, till the girl bows her head. No, she does not want to hurt her mother. No, she does not want people to be scared. No, she does not want to be hated.

After that, her mother keeps her in the house. Calls it home-schooling, but they both know better. The girl stares out of the bedroom window, watches children playing on the street. When she weeps, her mother says, "You can go out when you've learned to control yourself."

She stifles herself into obedience. Stamps out the smallest flicker before it has time to swell. Rolls up her radiance and shoves it inside her ribs, where it throbs, bangs on her walls. Her skin erupts along the fault lines, and eczema scores truth across her body.

At night, she goes into the yard and buries herself up to the neck in sand. It's the only way to keep her mother safe. She seethes in nightmares where she scours a world of ash, searching for people like herself. She promises herself this is only till she's old enough to leave. Her mother must be wrong. The world will love her light. She'll find fiery sisters, brothers, and build new constellations, stringing stars around the earth. She counts the days.

She grows, leaves home. Boys come: they love her party tricks of lighting candles with her fingers, singeing their eyebrows, breathing fire. They gawp at the glow of her nipples, the lava of her tongue. Crumple their noses when she tells them it's safe to touch the hungry magma between her thighs. They hold her at arm's length. Don't hold her at all.

Girls come: they tip their heads to one side, listening for the cracks through which to slide knives. They sneer at her selfishness. She ought to be ashamed for taking up so much room. It's not how good girls should behave. She should step down, step back. Dial down her glitter, stop showing off, stop dazzling her light in everybody's eyes.

She meets no-one to match her shimmer. Stops going to parties. Stops returning calls. Stops going out. Just stops. She's had years to perfect the skill of imprisoning her illumination. Keeps moving, from city to unlit city. Whenever she slips and shows a bit of sparkle, she moves on again.

But it's hell to rein in fire if all you are is flame. One night, her restraint buckles, breaks. She unbolts the door at 4am and runs to the heart of town. Climbs to the top floor of the car park and stretches out upon the deck, with only sky to cover her. She unlocks the mouth of her furnace. They haven't spoken for so long that at first all she can hear are whispers, staccato soft: syllables popping like anxious corks. But it swells, unrolls wild tongues in a wave that builds to a crest that can no longer be contained. She bursts. She blazes. Lets loose the fireworks of her body, cascading upwards into the night. If she's the only burning girl in the whole world, then it's time to stop smothering her brightness.

Next morning, she wakes in a cooling pool of bitumen, unpeels herself and dashes to the stairs. She must escape before commuters come and nose their cars into the white-lined bays. At first, she thinks she's seeing things; that it's a trick played by the low angle of the sun. But there, and there, dotted across the deck. Scorched into the tarmac, the tell-tale shape of other bodies.

NO MATTER

The first time she takes any notice of science is the lesson on atomic structure. The nucleus, a speck of grit spun around with electrons, and every single one of them behaving unpredictably. She learns there's no such thing as solid: not textbook, chair, body.

She's always felt on the verge of flying apart, the earth uneasy beneath her feet. She gets queasy with panic: is there something wrong with her? Turns out all she's been feeling is atomic whirl. It is the solution to her equation, her $x = x$. She is made of movement, particles in a giddy rush around a tiny core. She feels it there, quietly exerting its minute gravity.

She is not quite nothing.

Quickly, before anyone notices, she shields herself with protective boredom. Scrawls answers with enough mistakes to get a low mark and slip beneath the radar.

She walks home swirling with knowledge. Delivers polite answers to *how-was-school;* hides in her room. Stripped of the day's distracting thump and clatter, she stretches across her bed, house fluttering around her, skin barely able to hold her in. She is unsure if the trembling in her limbs is the turbulence of protons and neutrons, or power. She thinks it is power.

She listens to the dance of electrons; discovers she can tune herself to its particular quiver. All the solidities she took for granted. It takes the slightest adjustment to align her empty spaces with those of the wall. She watches her fingers sink into the gap between the atoms of brick and mortar, feels a tingling like tongue-tip on a battery. Manages to slide wrist-deep before her courage falters and she withdraws.

It's going to take practice. When she's got it right, she will walk into the wall. There is a future to explore. An out-there she can't prove, but hopes is no place like home.

WAITING FOR TIME TO CATCH UP

When he goes downstairs, his mother is not in the kitchen. She's not in the bathroom or the yard either. He stands on the kerb and calls her name. The noise echoes from the walls of the houses along the street. He shouts till he's bored, but nobody comes to see what the fuss is about.

He walks to school, to laugh at his friends doing maths tests and getting told off by Mr Beedling. It doesn't take as long as expected and he wonders why his mother drives him every day, considering she's always in a snappy mood. The playground is empty, classrooms deserted.

He spends the day searching and finds no-one; not in houses, churches, shops, offices. He switches on his phone. The screen is a wash of static, as is his computer. He wonders where everyone's gone. Wonders if he should be scared.

Millions of people, taken somewhere they can't bother him.

At the local supermarket, he fills a basket with crisps and fizzy pop. Walks out without paying. There's nobody to pay. He goes to bed when he feels like it, gets up when he feels like it. No-one shouts: *do your homework, wash your hands, brush your teeth, sit up straight*.

In the mirror over the fireplace, he sees his family on the other side of the glass. Waves, but they don't notice. His mother comes close, fixing her makeup. He sticks out his tongue.

He doesn't bother changing into clean clothes. He can't figure out the washing machine and that's the excuse he'll use when this is all over and his mother asks why he's wearing the same filthy t-shirt. He eats in front of the television. It fizzes white noise, but still. Whoever said crisps are fattening was stupid.

Every now and then, he catches ghostly shadows in a shop window. He doesn't bother to turn. He knows they won't be there.

The grandfather clock his dad's so proud of ticks away the seconds. He spends a lot of time looking into the mirror. His father grows a beard. His mother does something with her hair. A picture of himself appears in a gilt frame on the wall. That school photo he hated.

"Am I dead?" he asks the woman in the looking-glass. She can't hear him.

He doesn't feel dead. He wonders if he's moved sideways, like Dr Who in the Tardis.

Something he used to call time passes. He writes down his name and those of his family and friends. There are gaps he can't remember how to fill. He doesn't grow out of his clothes. He wears the same body; the people in the mirror don't. His father shaves off the beard, grows sideburns. The room changes: new sofa and carpet, walls painted a different colour. A cot appears. Some nights, the skin between worlds is so thin he can hear crying.

He never thought he'd get bored of biscuits.

One afternoon, he comes home from wandering the streets and finds the mirror-lounge stacked with boxes labelled *kitchen, bathroom*. His father points at the looking-glass as though saying: *Do you want to keep this old thing?*

His mother presses her lips together, the way she does when making up her mind.

SELF-POSSESSED

What would you do differently if you had your life again?

The world's most pointless question. Second chances don't happen, and certainly not to a guy like you, who has never taken a chance he could avoid. And yet, here you are, being given precisely that: a chance. God knows it's a gift you don't deserve. You've wasted your life frittering away each possibility of happiness with dogged persistence. All because you could not – would not – accept the simple fact of who and what you are. You still can't say the word.

No, scratch that. Silence was the problem all along. If you'd said it from the start, out and proud, things would be different. *Gay.*

Here you are: an afternoon on the boat with Father and Mother, forty years ago. You wonder why this ordinary day is the one chosen to put things right. Why not something dramatic, a showstopper occasion you could grab hold of and say, *Yes. This is when things went wrong.*

There's no time to work out an answer. All you know is this is it. There won't be another opportunity. You are shoved back, shouldering the decades aside. Something tweaks the chambers of your heart and you fall into your young body so fast it makes you dizzy.

The boat rocks gently. You're at the stern, on beer and soda duty. Your father is pretending to fish, your mother pretending to read. So much pretending. No wonder you learned how to be a sham. You had great teachers. You watch your sixteen-year-old self lift the lid of the cooler and pause, his hand – your hand – hovering above crushed ice. You have to break through, have to get his attention. Now, before he fetches Mother one of those diet colas she claims to enjoy. Before she pats his cheek, testing it for stubble, cooing, *You'll always be my baby boy!* Before Father yells, *It's your fault the boy's a cissy!* and he shakes his mother off. Before he begins to toughen. Then it will be too late.

The chill of part-melted slush as he dives in. Sudden cold shoots up his arm and you make him lose his grip. You sense youthful puzzlement. *It's not like me to drop things. Goddamn*, he mutters, but under his breath, because Mother has a secret tracking system capable of detecting the faintest curse.

He flexes his fingers, works blood back in. Dammit, you're even thinking the thoughts of your teenage self: how you need a few scars to roughen up your knuckles, because Father sneers at your hands, elegant as your artistic uncle's. Father says, *artistic* with a mincing lisp and Mother laughs her flowery laugh and says, *oh Bill.*

You want to tell this young man not to blame himself for the slip, for the way he doesn't fit his father's picture of a man, for the way his mother keeps a bottle filled with clear liquor in her nightstand, and slops an inch into every soda. To stop blaming himself for everything. The words hover between your mind and his. There is so much to say.

Suddenly, you don't know where to begin. Maybe you ought to start confessing the mistakes you've made, warn him that he'll make them too if he doesn't change. Maybe you should describe your soulless apartment with its clean white furniture, blank wooden floors and empty bed, where you lie awake at 4am wondering how to fill the days, and the walls staring down with no answers. Warn him he'll end up there as well. Most of all, you need to tell him about the loneliness.

"Don't—" you begin, trail off. "Try—" you say, but that's not right. "Always—" No. "Never—" Surely not.

His young mouth turns down in a frown. *Goddamn*, he says, voice firmer. You must hurry. Your only chance to change must not end this way.

Start somewhere, you think. *Anywhere. But start*. Mother is calling for her drink. Above, the flicker of birds; below, the water flocking with fish. You threw away four decades hammering your square peg into the round hole the world told you was right and proper. A man does not need to corral a wild life within other people's rules and expectations.

You cannot, will not fail again.

"Open your eyes," you say, at last. "Be who you are. Take pride in all your unfitting pieces. There's nothing wrong with you, there never was."

He pauses. Pushes the hair out of his eyes.

"Do something foolish," you say. "Something different. Right now."

He looks around. You feel his anxiety tangle its knot, tight and tighter.

"Small steps," you say gently. "Take off your pants and jump. Dive in. Let the water shock you awake. Swim to the other shore. I'll be with you every step of the way. Through the beat-downs, the bullying. I'll be with you on the bus out of this pretty prison you call home. Through the doubt, when you think you'll never find a friend. Through the bad days and to the good. Let's do it right this time. And if not right, then better. You are not alone."

THE RED GLASSES

After signing the contract for possession of the spectacles, she's in a hurry to get back home. At the front door, she pauses to adjust the frames into a comfortable position. Cheap plastic by the look of them. She'd smirked at the pinkish tint to the lenses, as though they could fool her with that old one. *Rose-tinted, my eye.* But the promises were a different matter. She turns the key and steps inside.

The kitchen looks the same. After the hard sell, she was expecting new cabinets, a flashy cooker and expensive tiling. But here are the same cheap units, worktop swollen from continual spills from the kettle, the door under the sink dented from where someone kicked it. Through the window, the apple tree still oozes sap from the honey aphid infestation. Of all the... She's been had.

The front door opens and closes. Right on cue, Bill calls out his unnecessary, *"I'm home!"*

As if it was going to be anyone else. She doesn't reply. All those guarantees of life transformed beyond her wildest dreams. Going by the kitchen, he'll be another disappointment. She's such a fool.

When she finally turns to greet him, she can't repress a sharp breath. His slack stomach has sucked back into itself, his chin has shed five years of lazy fat, and the soft bags beneath his eyes have disappeared. As he leans down and places his briefcase next to the door, the seams of his shirt strain against the bulge of muscle.

He straightens back up and gives her a look she can't remember, before realising it's because he's never looked at her like that. Ever. It's the hunger of a secret lover who has rushed to be at her side, as though this is the first night they've had to themselves for weeks.

"Darling," he purrs.

He takes a step forward. She's pulled into the heat that radiates from him, strong as sunshine from that Greek holiday before they were married and she still believed. He smoothes her cheek with gentle fingertips, teases a strand of hair from behind her ear.

"New glasses?" he asks.

She doesn't tell him where she got them, nor how they're suddenly worth every single thing she signed away. He presses his mouth to hers, knocking the frames so that they dig into her eyebrows.

"Yes," she mumbles, through the kiss.

He pulls away. "Last thing I want to do is hurt you, my princess," he says with a wolfish grin, and slides the glasses off her nose.

She blinks. Far worse than the jowls that have reappeared, his features have sickened into the expression of a man who's bitten into an apple and tasted mould.

"I…" he begins, and stumbles away.

She wrestles the glasses back on.

A breath, and he's perfect once more. He brushes his lips across her forehead.

"I'm such a lucky guy," he says. "You're a dream come true."

The next day, he calls the office and takes her shopping instead. Anything she wants, he flashes his gold card, and it's hers. The day after that is a stroll along the river with dinner at that waterside pub, the pricey one.

"But darling," she protests, only half-meaning it. "Don't you have to go to work?"

"Work can take care of itself," he grins, waving the waiter over and ordering champagne. "Especially now I'm director of my own company."

"Director? I thought you —"

She closes her lips tight, to stop the old world creeping out. This is the truth, now. Every night, and plenty of afternoons as well, he sweeps her into his arms and carries her upstairs, without the slightest hint of breathlessness. Bout after passionate bout of sex, not the half-hearted going-through-the-motions she'd had to put up with. She keeps the glasses on the whole time. Especially in bed.

Later that week, she's sorting through his pockets before filling the washing machine. Old habits die hard. When she finds the receipt from the fancy jeweller on the High Street, her stomach rolls over. She reads *heart-shaped locket, 18 carat, with chain*. A delivery address on the other side of town. Another woman's name: Felicity. A memory stirs: Bill's interminable office party a couple of Christmases ago, him introducing a Felicity, the way his eye wandered. She'd suspected there was something going on, but doubted he had it in him.

She looks up. The glasses are on the bedside table. The red frames glint, taunting, *what did you expect without us?* She trips on the rug in her hurry to grab them. Through the lenses, the receipt reads *heart-shaped locket, 18 carat, with chain*. New words appear, unscrolling along the dotted line: *To be engraved, My Dear Wife, With Eternal Love*.

She removes the glasses: Felicity's name reappears. She puts them on again: her own name shimmers into its rightful position. Bill is hers now, and she has a better deal than this Felicity could have dreamed of. Life is perfect and is going to stay that way. Even so, she decides it's time she had a maid. Someone to do the laundry, and everything else while they're at it.

When Bill presents her with the locket, she manufactures surprise.

"What a wonderful gift!" she coos, swinging the gold heart like a pendulum.

He smiles. "Anything for you. As if I could look at another woman." His breath warms her ear. "Let's go crazy," he whispers, rustling a sheet of paper. "I checked us in online. Grab your bag. The Paris flight leaves in a few hours."

*

Two weeks later, after a particularly adventurous night of lovemaking, she lies in bed, listening to his breath. He no longer snores, of course. She wraps the chain of the locket around her fingers, unable to sleep, wondering about the woman it was meant for, in a different life. She knows she should leave it be, but a worm is gnawing at the core of her heaven.

Felicity. The name means happy. *Who's happy now?* she thinks. Felicity took her husband, but that was before. As she lies awake, it occurs that Felicity had the old Bill: dowdy, indecisive and flabby. Makes no difference. Her Bill is incomparably better, and Felicity doesn't have so much as a scrap.

After Bill leaves for work – because even company directors need to attend important meetings – she looks up Felicity's address online. Plots the fastest route across town. Something stirs in her memory, from the time she signed the contract: *take only what is yours*. She's not taking anything. Bill is hers. This is curiosity. To revel in what can't hurt her. The word *revenge* dangles out of reach.

She parks across the road. Waits almost an hour before the door opens and a small woman creeps out. As though she has picked up a scent, Felicity raises her head, face twisting into fear when their eyes meet. She opens the car door, gets out and strides up the path. Felicity shrivels away.

"Look at you," she hisses, backing her up against the wall.

Felicity's eyes stretch in a frightened startle. She's standing so close she can see miniature reflections of herself.

"What do you want?"

"I don't need a thing from you," she growls. "I've got everything. You hear? Everything."

She swells with grubby triumph. She's still curious. On a whim, she removes the glasses. Felicity blooms, as though love has blown life into her. A man comes out of the house, pushing a baby buggy. It's Bill, but not the old Bill. It's the shining new prince of her dreams. *But he's mine*, she thinks. His expression is what finishes her off: a man in love, not in lust.

She fumbles the glasses back on, almost dropping them in her hurry. Bill and the child wink out, and Felicity shrinks back into her cower. She races back to the car, grinds it into reverse and screeches home in half the time it took to get there. At every red light, women seem to be dragging children across the road. She squints at them through lenses smeared in an afterimage of Felicity's happy family. She rubs and rubs but can't get rid of it. She doesn't care. Hell, she can get any man she wants. She doesn't have to settle for Bill. The world is hers.

Bill won't be back for a while, and she's glad of the time to compose herself and clean the gunk off the glasses. She heads upstairs, opens the wardrobe and breathes relief when she sees Bill's shirts and jackets. Nothing has changed.

As she watches, they melt into nothing. A single wire hanger rocks backwards and forwards. His bedside table is clear, his shoes vanished. But she's wearing the glasses. She takes them off and the room looks the same. She puts them back on. No difference. She catches her face in the mirror on the dressing-table: sour lines drawn from nose to mouth, mean eyes.

It takes two to make a failure, whispers a voice she recognises. *Bill was not the only one who stopped making an effort.*

She can see something over her shoulder. She runs, slamming the bedroom door. Behind her, she hears the thump and crash of glass. This isn't what they promised. It's not fair. Her phone rings.

The terms were clear, says the voice. *Take only what is yours.*

"I wasn't taking anything!" she cries.

31

The laughter that trickles out of the earpiece is sticky and unpleasant. She ends the call, switches the phone off. The lenses have grown cloudier, as though the room is ghosted with fog. Try as she might, she can't remember the exact details of the contract. They were in such a hurry getting her to sign – the pen growing hotter and hotter in her fingers – and the lights were too dim to read the small print.

She tells herself there's nothing to worry about. It's not like their sort of contract would be binding in any court of law. That scratching at the window is just the wind blowing a branch of the apple tree against the glass. She'll get it cut down tomorrow, nasty diseased thing. She can have anything she wants. Anything. The glasses are hers. Nothing and nobody are taking them away.

AN EEL CAN PRODUCE ITS OWN BODY WEIGHT IN SLIME TO WRIGGLE OUT OF A TIGHT SITUATION

Over breakfast, we're sipping coffee when an eel flops out of your mouth. You try to poke it back in, but it looks me in the eye, wriggles off the table and out of the kitchen, greasy-fast. I think of that film where the alien bursts out of a man's chest in an explosion of gore. Here, there's not a drop.

"No blood," you gargle, cheerful for someone who's just regurgitated an eel. "And I'm not dead!"

You always know what I'm thinking.

You hawk, spit goo into a tissue. Slime drips from your fingers, pools on the floor at your toe-tips. You peer through your eyelashes, hair flopping over your brow, your favourite coy-boy expression slathered across your features.

"You promised this would never happen again," I say.

I march to the sink, skidding in your drool but making a quick recovery. I turn the tap on full blast and wring a cloth into a strangle. Get on my knees to swab the floor. Once again, I'm the one clearing up your mess.

A year ago, it was pork products. You'd come home late from the office and throw up. Mother told me it'd run its course and it did, after six months of incidents involving thin-sliced ham, sausages, and one time a gammon steak so huge I was dialling for an ambulance when you grabbed the phone and yelled, *'Stop being so sodding dramatic!'*

I shouldn't have let it slide. Should have stared down your excuses: something you ate, probably that tapas bar you went to with the guys after work and never got home till after two, stinking of yeast and salt. I should have been less understanding when you started sleeping on the couch so as not to disturb me.

You're still coughing while I mop the puddle at your feet. It ought to have the stinging odour of vomit. Instead, I catch the familiar whiff of yeast and salt, homely and unmistakeably female. I get to my feet, inspect you for clues. You shove me away when I get too close.

"Rockets to the moon, vaccines, quantum theory, and we still don't know how eels have sex," you splutter, flashing the smile my mother calls *winning*.

I'm not thinking about eels, sex, rockets, or any of the other things you come up with, which proves you *don't* know what's on my mind. Never have done. A few lucky strikes and the rest is Houdini hooey, a grifter magician getting me to look the other way. You've greased your way out of a lie for the final time.

I'm thinking about how long I've known the truth, but kept hanging onto something that was slithering from my fingers. I'm calculating your chances of wriggling out of this one.

WHAT BUSINESS HAS A HORSE TO LOOK DOWN ON ME?

The horse is in the kitchen again. Beats me how, when I lock every door and window. I concentrate on washing up, grinding a scouring pad in circles to shift burnt-on rice. The horse shakes its head, flapping the damp velvet of its lips. I refuse to turn, because that would acknowledge its existence. It sneezes snot onto the tiled floor.

Snort all you like, buster, I think, attacking the pan with a knife.

My father said horses were God's most perfect creatures. *Steady and reliable*, he said, wrong in that piece of wisdom as he was in everything. The closest he got to steady was shedding his wages on a slow stumbler who fell at the first fence.

Cats are the best animal. They can squeeze under doors, climb curtains. No one can show me a horse clever enough to do that, not with their constant demands for attention, finicky appetites, rolling eyes. Cats taught me how to need no one, not ever.

The horse taps a hoof, muscles quivering along the russet sheen of its flanks. If I continue to ignore it, it will leave. I'm good at ignoring, like I ignore the memory of the last time I saw my father and the words we screamed at each other, burned hard on the inside of my skull like the rice on this pan.

They say the apple doesn't fall far from the tree. Depends how steep the slope. Soon as I could, I rolled down my hill, further and further away, picking up speed until apple trees and horses were less than specks of dirt in my eye, nothing a bit of salt water couldn't wash away.

I hurl the ruined pan into the bin and stride into the hall; button up my coat. The horse trots after, glances at my laced-up boots, shakes its mane coquettishly. If that's what it wants, it can have it. I open the door.

"Go on," I snarl. "Do us both a favour and sod off."

I'd say it's sulking but horses can't smile, or frown, or anything else that counts as an expression. I slam the door so forcefully I loosen the hinges. I shrug off the coat, head to the bathroom and slide the bolt. The horse is ahead of me. It leans against the bath, scenting the room with straw.

I've tried to work out when it first arrived. I'm sure I just came home one day and there it was, nose shoved in a box of teabags, but memories slide away when I attempt to cling too tightly.

It takes a clopping step, rests the massive block of its head on my shoulder. I won't buckle. Won't let it know I'm weighed down, because then I'd have to stop. I'd have to remember when I had dreams of walking into my first job and flying up the ladder. Friends and parties and open roads stretching to a horizon without hills and nothing to mess up the view.

The horse lets out a sigh, treacly and warm. It shouldn't be me who has to change. I asked for nothing, certainly not a horse following me around, flapping its huge eyelashes and making pitying noises at the back of its throat.

And if, just if, I put in all the hard work and thankless slog at sorting out my life, I'd have to stop slamming doors. I'd have to turn around and look the horse in the eye. I'd have to speak kind words, lay my arm around its neck, let it lead me out the back door and show me how the garden is bursting with new life this time of year and then who would be left to clear up all this shit?

LOOK BOTH WAYS

Everyone deserves an interesting exit. Better than a bare-gums, blurred-eyes, clenched-fingers drift into the void. I'm filling the tank with unleaded: shake the drops off the nozzle and drive out faster than the five miles per hour I'm supposed to stick to. I slow down on the sliproad. Stop and let him in, ignore his bleat of "*Birmingham, please?*" Later, when it's too late, I wonder whether he said that at all.

"Yeah," I say, not taking my eye off the white lines. "I hate the M6."

"Thanks for picking me up," he says.

"Yeah."

"I'd only been there five minutes."

"Yeah."

"My lucky day. I need one." He sniffs, picks at his cuffs.

"Downwardly mobile?"

"Pardon?"

"Should have said *what*. Posh types say *Pardon*."

"What?"

"That's better. Your camouflage isn't working. I spotted you a mile off."

His forehead corrugates. I tailgate four drivers hogging the middle lane at exactly seventy miles an hour. One by one they obey my flashing headlights and honking; huddle back into the inside lane.

"You said, *I hate the M6*," he says eventually.

"I do."

"But we're on the M1."

"So?"

"Um. Nothing."

"I haven't got a problem with the M1. You got a problem?"

"No."

"Good. What's that smell?"

"Pardon? What?"

"Are you smoking weed?"

"No!"

"Sure?"

"I don't smoke at all. It's a bad habit."

"Just don't smoke in my car, ok?"

"Ok."

I balance my fingertips on the rim of the steering wheel at ten to two.

"Driving instructors say *ten to two*. Why not *ten past ten*?"

"What?"

"Better."

"Uh?"

"Now you're getting it. Y'know. You said *what* when I asked a question. Then grunted. Even better."

I take the exit to Leicester Forest Services so fast we judder over the hatched-off area.

I giggle. "It makes my lip sweat, doing that."

"Christ," he squeaks, gripping the seat till his knuckles whiten. "You're not the only one. Is this *Deliverance* or something?"

"No. You sure *ain't* got a pretty mouth, boy." I laugh, banging the dashboard. "Go on, say it for me."

"What?"

"Got it in one. I like you." We get out of the car and I slap him on the back. He coughs the whole time it takes us to walk from the far end of the car park to the whooshing doors. I take the opportunity to tell him a story. "These services are the biggest pile of crap in this entire pile of crap we call a country. Bring back Thatcher," I say, sneaking a look at his response, but he's still hacking his lungs up. I'm lying about Thatcher, but all artists are liars. "Even worse than Watford Gap," I continue. "That song may have been true once, but not anymore."

He unbends, looks at me with watery eyes. "Song?" he wheezes.

"The song?" I gasp. "You don't know the song? Nothing like a good tune to cure a broken heart."

I power up as the doors open for us. I love a big entrance, as my grandfather used to say. *Watford Gap, Watford Gap, plate of grease and a load of crap.* I flick the ends of my footballer perm at the man selling RAC membership. He smiles back. A kid stares until its mother slaps its face sideways.

"Mum, why's that man got lady's hair?" it squeals.

"They can't help themselves," I say to my new friend. "Kids."

His head ducks: embarrassed. Suddenly, I hate the way people like him crawl under my skin. The reckless smile, the thoughtless happiness, the way he's young and can't wait to get older. Bile rises up my throat, before settling and trickling back down, sloshing against the walls of my stomach in an alkaline tide. Makes my knuckles go into overload. You could use me to clamp illegally-parked vehicles. I loathe him so loudly he must be able to hear.

"Don't say a word." I'm generous. I give warnings.

"I wasn't going to."

"That's four. Words."

The woman drags her brat towards the shop. It owls its head at me for as long as it can. I mime wringing necks and it finds its mother's skirt and takes a good long sniff.

"Tea," I say, filled with sudden, guilty affection. "I'm buying."

They only have doll-house size teapots, so I get us two each. I ask for real milk, not that shit in plastic thimbles, and the server looks like I'm asking for plutonium. My comradely warmth lasts the first pot and most of the way through the second. He's sipping from his cup like a sparrow.

"What the fuck's the matter with you?" I say it gently, but it still makes mouths purse up and children giggle.

"I just don't like the taste of tea," he whispers. "I'm sorry. Look, I'll just get another lift. Ok?"

He scrapes his chair back.

"I'm taking you."

"It's ok," he bleats. "Really."

"I said, I'm taking you. Don't rock the boat."

He's too weasel to make a big fuss. While he fiddles with his tea, I look around at bad-tempered families. To our right is a group of four children of indeterminate age, fighting and screaming while the mother ignores them, gawking at her mobile. On the table to our left, a boy starts to bawl. His father hunches over him, forefinger-and-thumb squeezes the tiny nostrils shut, clamps his palm over the gaping mouth. The wailing hiccups to a stop. Dad hangs on a few more seconds, then lets go. The kid's eyes dilate in moist adoration.

"I'm your only way out of here," I beam at my companion. "You know it." I look at him for a long, affectionate minute. "You finished?" I nod at his cup.

"Oh," he says. "Yes."

"You've got places to be."

"I'm in no hurry."

"Well, I am."

"Oh. Sure."

He follows me to the exit, pauses on the ribbed mat no-one is bothering to wipe their feet on. It has started to rain.

"You got something against water?" I growl.

"No. I just need to go to the toilet."

"I'll wait."

He's gone a long time.

"I couldn't go," he says.

The car welcomes us by opening the first time I point the electronic fob at it.

"It needs new batteries. These are fucked." I show my teeth to him so he knows it's a joke. "I worry about you," I say, as he slides into the passenger seat. "Like, you're not even putting on your seatbelt. *Clunk click*. Though you're too young to remember that one."

He fiddles with the strap. Stops. "Look," he says. "I need to walk around for a bit. Carsick."

I lean across him and snap the buckle shut. "I'm taking you to Birmingham."

"But we're on the M1."

We leave the car park and glide down the sliproad. *Mirror, signal, manoeuvre.*

"I want to get out," he whines, sliding his mobile out of his pocket. He's trying to be sly, and failing.

I pull onto the hard shoulder. Stretch over him and push the door open.

"You're not a prisoner. It's not like I've got handcuffs."

He snatches air in small tight puffs. His hands tremble so much he almost drops the phone. "It's raining," he says.

He crumples into a corner of himself. I wait for the length of time it would take to drink a can of cola, then pull the door closed. There is a scatter of raindrops on the inside of the window. I lower the window, grab his phone and toss it out.

"Why did you..."

"Right. Birmingham," I say, and put the car into gear. "It's a grand place when you get to know it."

"My phone..." he wails.

"Exactly. You feel better already, don't you?"

"I need it."

"No, you don't. Bane of the modern world."

He gulps, his eyes wide as fishponds. "Are you going to..." he says, voice trailing off.

"Kill you? Is that what you're thinking?" I tip back my head and roar. The car swings from lane to lane. "Not me. I leave that malarkey to the amateurs."

"Please," he whimpers. "Please."

As the car swerves back and forth, drivers lean on their horns. He starts to cry. I can't stop laughing at what he thinks of me. I'm not that kind of guy. I wouldn't leave a mark on his carefree, stupid head. There are far worse things than dying; rewards that linger more sweetly than the brief flare and gutter of murder. The motorway unrolls before us.

Birmingham. Manchester. Even Swindon. So many overlooked places in a city, even at its heart. People walking past, gabbling into their mobiles, unaware of what's happening five yards away.

"Wait and see what I have planned for us," I say. "I promise, it'll be unforgettable."

WHAT GOES ON IN THE BUSHES

I'm taking the shortcut through the park, when I see him under the stand of poplars. He is staring into the bushes, a dog leash minus its dog looped around his left wrist. I stroll across, swishing leaves with the toes of my boots, loud enough for him to hear. I don't like creeping up on people.

He doesn't stir.

"Lost your dog?" I say.

At first, I wonder if he's hard of hearing, but very slowly, he rotates his head until he's looking me in the eye. Just as slowly, he curves his mouth into a smile that stretches into a thin line. Without answering the question, he turns away and resumes his examination of the undergrowth.

He's there the following afternoon, the afternoon after. I try other conversational starters: squirrels, the weather, the way the council refuses to clean out the pond. He ignores me with great politeness. I stand beside him, hands shoved into my pockets, and concentrate on the same spot. It's just a bush: regular size, glossy leaves, no berries, no spider webs, nothing scurrying beneath. By the end of the week, I can't stand it any longer.

"I don't get it," I say.

He smiles his leisurely smile, raises his left hand and holds out the dog leash. He nods encouragingly, so I take it. He closes his eyes. Just when I think he's going to stay that way forever, he opens them and takes a step backwards. Then he turns around and strides away, picking up speed and disappearing into the trees. The dog leash is warm from his touch. I clutch it tightly, and stare into the bush. Children shout in the play area. Ducks quack on the pond. Magpies cackle above. Little by little, the tide of sound goes out. It gets dark. It gets light again.

It might be hours; it might be days. A man appears beside me.

"Lost your dog?" he says.

I turn and smile, very slowly. He doesn't understand, not yet. He will.

I'LL BE SEEING YOU

The first sighting is at the traffic lights. He drums the steering wheel, distracted by the hole in his glove where the fingertip is working its way out. On amber, he crunches the gears, ready for the off. As the lights turn green, a man hurtles across the road. Hair past the shoulders, gaudy shirt. He'd not be seen dead in a shirt like that; hair like a girl.

The man twists his head mid-gallop and grins. Their eyes meet, and he realises he's looking at himself. Not a vague lookalike, but a perfect replica: nose, eyes, chin, even the tilt of the head. He stalls the engine, to an angry fanfare of horns. Rubs his eyes until green-orange ghosts haunt the back of his eyelids. When his vision clears, the man has vanished. He tells himself it must have been a trick of the light; glare bouncing off the windscreen.

For the rest of the drive home, his fingers cramp from gripping the wheel. The man might have been his double, but the hairstyle and shirt were far too daring. No, not daring: idiotic. As a youth, he sneered when others got themselves gussied up like peacocks; sniggered behind their backs, as they partied from Saturday to Saturday without a break. Fools who wasted their summers backpacking through Europe, getting jobs in unpronounceable places halfway across the world. He showed them. He's the one with the sensible job for over twenty years; who's almost paid off the mortgage; who has the perfect marriage.

When he turns onto his quiet street, he feels an odd sense of relief. It takes longer than it should for his breathing to even out. He fumbles with the house keys, drops them twice. A beetle is crawling across the doorstep. He stamps on it.

*

"And the shirt!" he says to his wife over dinner. "Floral!"

"So?"

"He looked like me," he mutters. He can't tell her the truth; the man *was* him down to the last detail. "A bit. You know."

"I don't," she replies.

He prods the sac of the poached egg and it oozes yellow. Wednesday is the day for egg and chips. Today is Tuesday. He doesn't understand why his wife has caused this unnecessary disruption. Tuesday is always shepherd's pie. No peas. He doesn't hold with peas, even if the recipe calls for them. *Diced carrot*, he said to his wife, after the honeymoon in Torquay. *Don't serve peas and we'll be fine.*

"Why are we having egg and chips?"

She shrugs, dunks a chip in a blob of ketchup, bites it in half.

"But it's Tuesday." He pokes a chip with his fork. "Is this about the diced carrot?"

"Is what about diced carrot?"

"Dinner. Tuesday. Shepherd's pie. I know you resent me for not eating peas."

"Peas?"

"Peas! You're not paying attention."

"I always pay attention."

She doesn't sound sarcastic. He decides to change the subject.

"Have you done something with your hair?"

"No," she says, mopping up yolk with a piece of bread.

Second time is on the motorway sliproad. The man who has stolen his face is leaning on a car and laughing into a phone. Not any car: his car, even the licence plate. He's still wearing the moronic clothes and flamboyant haircut. They lock eyes and the youth waves as if to an old friend.

He grasps the wheel like a lifebelt. The seam on his glove tears a little wider.

All the way home, he's convinced he can see his own car in the rear-view mirror, following. He is definitely seeing things. He sticks out his tongue, cranes his neck to check in the rear-view mirror and almost drives into the central reservation. He pulls up on the hard shoulder, heart pounding. He must have eaten something that disagreed with him. Maybe the eggs were off. And he's been sleeping badly. His wife says he snores, and that snoring damages the heart. She's always—

She—

She—

He can't catch hold of her name. This is ridiculous. He wipes the mirror, smearing the glass. His forehead is shimmering, clammy to the touch. Further proof he's ill.

He opens the front door to be greeted by the smell of roast chicken. *Roast chicken is Sunday*, he wants to yell. His wife is halfway through a glass of white wine. He grabs the bottle, pours one for himself. His hands are shaking. He never drinks on a weekday. Then again, neither does she. She's wearing a top with ruffles around the neckline. He'd swear it's the same fabric as the man's shirt.

"That's a new blouse, isn't it?" he asks, fighting to keep his voice steady.

"No," she says, staring him down.

Whatever she says, there *is* something different about her. Hair? Shoes? Makeup? He must be careful what he says next.

"I didn't buy it for you."

"No, you didn't."

"I buy all of your clothes."

"No, you don't."

She looks younger, relaxed, surer of herself. The word *happy* comes into his head. Of course she's happy, he thinks. There's never been a happier marriage. They're perfect for each other.

"Why are you being like this?"

"Like what?"

"You know very well what I mean."

She doesn't answer. Her expression is blank. Nothing for him to seize on. She glides away. He battles the urge to scream, *I didn't say you could leave!* He has no idea why he's so unsettled. He takes a glug of wine and notices he's left no fingerprints on the glass. He rubs his thumb against the side. Not a mark. That night, he lies awake, listening to his wife breathing. He wants to reach out, tell her he's being eaten alive by something he can't explain. He doesn't know how to start. They've never been that sort of couple.

Third time is the Chinese takeaway on the corner. He's putting in an order for sweet and sour chicken, when his young and handsome self shoves the door open. He tries to hide by examining the menu taped to the wall.

"Well, if it isn't...!" blares the impostor.

He has no choice but to turn round. The man sticks out a hand, little finger glinting with the signet ring his wife gave him on his birthday. His own fingers are bare.

"You've stolen my——" he starts, stuttering to a halt.

"Look who's here!" shouts the man. "It's old..."

Old what? he thinks. *I'm not old, I'm just...*

His wife materialises at the man's shoulder.

"Oh, it's you," she says, in the voice she uses at office parties when she can't remember the name of the person she's been introduced to. His order of sweet and sour chicken is called. His twin-not-twin scoops it up.

"But that's mine," he whines.

48

They put their arms around each other and squeeze tight. The connection when they look at each other makes the air hum.

"Let's go dancing," she purrs.

His wife hates dancing. Hates it. He shakes his head.

"Anything for you, Anna," says the doppelganger.

Anna! Of course. He didn't forget her name. It slipped momentarily, that's all. Yes, his wife's called... His mind is a void. He grinds his teeth, willing her name to come back.

"Why is this happening?" he moans.

The thief leans close.

"She's slipped through your fingers," he murmurs. "Like your hopes and dreams. You let them go, each and every one. Ready and waiting for someone to pick them up and make them come true."

He had dreams. How dare this charlatan suggest he didn't. But dreams are for children and he put that nonsense away when he grew up, like any sane person. After all, if you don't have hopes, you can never be disappointed. Nothing wrong with cautious and careful. He has a great life. Steady job, steady wife. That's what matters, he tells himself. If only he could remember her name.

"This isn't fair," he whines. "What did I do?"

The man whispers, "Nothing."

"I don't understand..."

"Let me put it this way. What didn't you do? Everything. I'm simply living your life to the full. You didn't."

Despite the stuffy heat inside the takeaway, a chill runs down the back of his neck. He runs a finger around the inside of his shirt collar, moist with sweat.

"What now?" he says, wiping his nose on his sleeve. "You've taken my life, my wife, even my order of sweet and sour chicken. Going to bump me off, eh? Eh?"

The man smiles and shakes his head fondly. "Don't worry. You have the life you wanted. Safe. Quiet. Unremarkable." He pats him on the arm, gently. "No one will notice you've gone."

"No," he wheezes. His heart is pattering so lightly he can hardly hear it.

The pair stroll out of the takeaway and onto the street. He catches his reflection in the plate glass. Stooped shoulders, thinning hair, swollen knuckles. *That can't be me in the window,* he thinks. *Not at all.*

"I'm happy, I tell you!" he squeaks. "No regrets. Not one!"

The man he could have been starts up the car and edges away from the kerb. He lurches after, grabs the handle of the driver's door. It won't open. He bangs on the window. His wife is smiling as he's never seen her smile.

"I love you!" he yelps, frantic.

The car accelerates, driving away with his future.

"Help me!" he pipes, falling at the side of the road and rolling into the gutter. "He's stolen everything!" A beetle picks its way towards him, antennae quivering. The sound of its tiny claws is deafening. "Please," he pipes, voice a quavering whisper that trickles down into the drain.

The weekend crowds step over him and walk on, unseeing and unhearing.

LOW SEASON

"That's our table."

I slide my attention away from the window, over the bulging overhang of the man's stomach and up towards his face. A wife cowers at his shoulder, rumpled as a pillowslip. I stretch my broadest smile, the one Mother said could make a cat laugh.

"Good morning, sir," I say, raising my cup in a toast.

It's how conversations should begin. I take a sip of coffee, unexpectedly fine for this moderately-priced bed and breakfast. I've stayed in places three times the price and been served swill.

"We sit there," continues the man, snapping each word like a twig when he's finished with it.

I can see why he likes it. It's the only table with a view. I gaze at the sea: lines of wooden posts are marching into the water; grey waves fold their lace border onto the sand's edge, the continual rustling of a sheet being pulled from a mattress.

"Don't we?" he says, louder.

The wife glances from husband to me with birdlike twitches of the head.

"I'll be gone as soon as I've finished my coffee," I say.

The only other occupants of the breakfast room are a couple in the far corner, pretending they aren't watching.

"You've seen me!" growls the man, in their direction. "Every morning. For a week. At this table!"

They stare at their plates.

"I was told I could sit anywhere," I say, leaning back in my chair.

A waitress appears, takes one look at the standoff, executes a neat spin and vanishes through the swing doors.

"You! Woman!" he bellows. In the kitchen, a radio is turned up loud. The man flushes from the neck up, grips the corner of my table between thumb and forefinger. "You don't bother me, pal," he splutters.

His fingernails are ragged, gnawed to the quick. I examine my own perfect manicure: crescent moons rising from smooth nail beds, the tips free of the white flecks Mother called *gifts*.

The wife takes a step towards the door. He fires her a look and she folds in half as though shot, with a gasping hiss echoing the faint brush of waves. I wonder if she is going to hyperventilate. Although fascinating to observe, I decide not to enquire. In these situations, wives are unreliable.

She blinks. "He does like this table," she whispers. "You understand, don't you?"

The man leans forward, slams his hands down. My cup jiggles. I breathe in, spread my palms flat upon the cloth. The linen has been ironed by a careless hand. If I pressed the tablecloth, I would do a wonderful job. The management would be delighted. But I have made promises to the authorities. Have surrendered many desires.

"You," he squeaks, mouth opening and closing with a popping sound. "You."

If I stood, he would see in my eyes what lies within. Wisely, I remain seated. Take a slow mouthful of coffee. I am required to answer. It is the done thing. But I'm mesmerised by his puppet show: grinding teeth, pounding fists, blustering complaints. With each passing minute his face grows redder, as though he is pumping up his head like a balloon.

"Sorry," says the wife, chin jabbing backwards and forwards, a pigeon pecking at gravel.

I could leave. Could take this excellent coffee to my room and enjoy it overlooking the compulsive sea. But that kind of thing never ends well. However hard I try, I am not comfortable in cramped rooms with cramped beds, where the sheets become unruly despite my lying with arms clamped to my sides. Here, where the tablecloth is obedient and people are watching, I can be still. See. My hands are barely trembling.

The man advances until his stomach is an inch from my face. I can smell how long since his trousers were dry-cleaned. The wife picks up a serviette and worries it between her fingers, earning such a scowl from her husband she hurls it away as though it's on fire.

"You're done here," he squeals. "Get out. Now."

There have been other occasions. Incidents I have been instructed not to dwell upon. Unhealthy incidents. I could tell him I've sworn to practice restraint. Have sworn to sleep in a bed all night and not remake it with fresh linen on the hour, every hour. I could tell him of the things I can achieve with a steam iron on its highest setting. With my left hand I crack the knuckles of my right, to stop it getting ideas.

He doesn't hear the warning.

"I'm sorry," tweets the wife.

I don't know if she's apologising for him, or for what she can see brewing in my hands and face. I have made assurances, I remind myself. Have signed papers, crisp folds dividing each page into equal parts.

He is making noises partway between speaking and grunting. His face doesn't know what to do. It can't flush a deeper puce, having gone as far as it can. His scraggy neck has swollen to fit the collar. Clever, I think, to give himself room to manoeuvre.

I drain my cup, set it down gently. Tell myself a restless sea and rumpled linen are part of the natural order. I will not find answers by pressing everything into submission. Disarray is healthy, and I can begin with small quantities, such as one might measure in teaspoons. I have to remember so many difficult things.

I turn to the man and smile. He looks at me and does not.

For the final time, I gaze at the brimming tide. Its ragged hem is tearing itself to shreds, ripping out its tidy stitches. I grit my teeth.

I must not think of things that can be twisted into a gasping strangle.

Must not forget my agreement, the endless clauses.

Must not forget all of my promises.

Must not.

WHAT BECOMES OF THE NIGHT WHEN THERE IS NOTHING LEFT TO SEE?

He arrives early as usual, so there is time to polish the desk and filing cabinet with lemon-scented spray. He checks the pinboard for announcements, the blue hessian a patchwork of lighter and darker squares from notices long-gone. He unlocks the filing cabinet with the little key he wears around his throat – the drawer squeaking on its runners – and removes a fresh sheaf of squared paper. Only then does he winch the blinds shut and adjust the viewer for observation mode.

He begins in the north-east quadrant. Moving clockwise, he greets stars as old friends: Rigel, Antares, Betelgeuse. Not that he ignores insignificant lights known only by number. To him, the small are as important as the great. He imagines himself crossing the ballroom of the sky to where dim wallflowers cower and, with a smile, leading them into the dance of constellations.

Sector by sector, he continues in a steady rhythm: counting and recording, counting and recording. In one of his training modules, he read how one square centimetre of the sky contains 100,000 galaxies. It was the moment he fell in love with the night and she became his one true mistress. As he makes the first cup of tea of many, he imagines this job as a nightly rushing into her arms. It is a fanciful indulgence; one he only permits in secret. He squeezes the teabag and deposits it in the small brass container set aside for that purpose.

The hours unroll deliciously. He always looks forward to the half-hour just before dawn. Not because it signals the end of his shift when he can tick the box marked *all present*, but for the sight of Scorpio rising in the east. One is not supposed to have favourites.

There: partway down the tail. He cleans his spectacles on the little yellow cloth he keeps in his breast pocket and looks again. Girtab has vanished.

He wipes the viewfinder. Pinches the bridge of his nose. Looks again, but the blue giant has not reappeared. He wishes he could blame the bronze glow of coming sunrise, but it is impossible. For the first time in twenty-three years of service, he completes a Missing Star Report Form: *Sector 32271. 04.32. Girtab. Not present.*

Usually, he enjoys the tram ride home against the tide of bleary workers beginning their day's labours. The restful clack-clack of the wheels, the familiar calling-out of the stations in a countdown to his own. This morning it brings no pleasure. He phones his sister, who lives in the southern part of the city.

"Girtab has disappeared," he says. "It's a star," he adds, hastily.

"How do you know?" she asks, after a pause.

"Because it isn't there."

"No need to snap. It's probably cloudy." He grasps the receiver tightly, not trusting himself to answer politely. In the background he hears a thud, followed by the squeak of a child. "Are you still there?" his sister asks, as the squeak spirals into a wail. "Look, I have to get the children to school. I'm sure there's nothing to worry about. Let's talk soon. Yes?"

The line clicks, already dead.

"Mother always preferred you!" he cries into the silent mouthpiece.

He's taken aback. He is not a man given to outbursts. Despite tincture of valerian, he cannot sleep. He stares at the ceiling, waiting for an agitated phone call from the Ministry, demanding an explanation and accusing him of some foolish prank.

That evening, he rushes to the observatory. The stack of reports from the night before have been collected, but there are no fresh instructions, no acknowledgment of his missing star.

Unsure what else to do, he cleans the furniture. It is clotted with a thick layer of dust, despite his assiduous attentions the previous evening. He switches on the equipment and begins the night's first notations. Everything is where it should be. His breath steadies, until he moves north-west.

Cygnus has lost part of a wing. Two minor lights, barely magnitude 4, but a star is a star, however unimpressive. He fills in a second report form. Cleans his glasses. Blows his nose. Stares at the phone. He lifts the receiver and calls Head Office, using the emergency number pinned to the notice board. A recorded voice asks him to leave a message.

"Girtab has gone," he says, hearing the idiocy of the statement. "Cygnus is losing his wings."

A week passes. There are no calls from the Ministry, nothing in his in-tray. Each night is marked by further loss. On Tuesday, Taurus sheds a horn; Wednesday, Orion his sword. By Thursday the Pleiades have dwindled to four sisters; by Friday, three. He writes report after report in red ink studded with exclamation marks.

"Is no one listening?" he screams into the phone. "Why don't you answer? Don't any of you care?"

The weekend stretches before him, long and silent. He trims his moustache and eyebrows. As the inhabitants of his apartment block prepare burdensome evening meals, he makes a light repast of coffee and warmed rolls. He trims the hair from his ears and nostrils. Sews a loose button on his shirt.

At sunset on Sunday, he decides to travel into the city and speak with the weekend shift worker. They will know what to do. And if they don't, at least the two of them can present a united front to the Ministry. He boards a tram, discomfited by the press of bodies, the intrusive chattering of those heading to bars where they will squander their time sipping wine. And so many children for this time of the evening, squabbling noisily over imagined slights – an apple unfairly divided, an extra sweet given to the other. As a boy he was courteous to his sister, scrupulously fair. He is relieved to disembark.

A concierge he does not recognise demands his identity card. She inspects it as though dealing with a thief, glancing from photograph to face over and over. He adjusts the sleeves of his jacket to conceal frayed shirt-cuffs. When she finally unlocks the gate, it is with an air of thwarted disappointment.

He dashes up the stairs. The door is locked. He has never needed a key: the office has always been open. The concierge refuses to give him a passkey. He demands. There is a cheerful refusal. He demands again. The concierge threatens to call the police. He has no option but to return to his apartment. He stops at the 24-hour grocery store and buys a can of soup.

"The stars are disappearing," he says to the young woman at the cash register.

"Aren't there hundreds of them?"

"Billions."

"Well, then," she says. "Won't miss a few."

She smiles politely, asks if he has a smaller note, as she is almost out of change.

On Monday evening, the office door is unlocked as usual. Upon his desk is a sheaf of Star Report Forms, neatly stacked, edges lined up in perfect formation. There is still no memorandum from Head Office in recognition of the momentous events of the past week. Ten minutes before the close of shift, the phone rings. He grabs the receiver, almost dropping it.

"What is your ministerial classification?" demands a voice, sounding mechanical as the answerphone.

"The stars are disappearing!" he cries. The words crack in the middle.

"What is your ministerial classification?" the voice repeats.

He fishes out his identity card and gabbles the string of numbers and letters. "What's happening to the stars?"

"Your observation reports have been received."

"What am I supposed to do?"

"Continue."

"Continue?"

"Your job description is clear. Observe. Notate. Record."

"But more are vanishing. Every night."

The line goes dead. His shift comes to an end. He files his reports. The tram seems emptier than usual, each passenger sitting as far as possible from their neighbour. He surveys his fellow travellers, seeking a bright eye, a flicker of eager interest, but their faces are blurred with placid discontent. He wonders how many stars will have to vanish before they notice. How many more before they care, and what will become of the night when there is nothing left to see?

He takes his tincture of valerian and climbs into bed. The following evening, he goes to work. What else can one man do? He observes. He notates. He records. He lists the missing.

THE ASTRONOMICAL MENAGERIE

The Comet prowls from wall to wall, flicking the plume of her tail. She ignores the climbing frame, the swing rope, the unbreakable mirror that fractures her expression. I keep up as best I can, swabbing pools of shed light so visitors don't slip and land us with a lawsuit. Despite the notices, they pound her window, laying bets on how long they can touch the glass before their fingers smoulder.

The brightness of her claws. The crackle of her mane. Her beard a river of fire. Back and forth, she flows. Her spittle sizzles potholes in the floor.

Why doesn't she play? they ask. *She has so many toys.*

She crawls to the corner where the arc light cannot reach, turns to the wall. They straggle out, complaining of migraines. They'll queue for hours to throw bread rolls for the Red Giant to incinerate mid-air; prefer meteor showers that perch upright, sparkling prettily.

The Comet cramps in space the shareholders have deemed sufficient. Every moment of every day, she grinds a rut, watching for a weakness in the fence.

At night, when the visitors have gone, she unravels. Inhales lungfuls of universe; spills it out. Fills every square inch of her enclosure, could fill a million more.

I hide her discarded radiance in bottles, take it home and wash my hair. Scrub my limbs with her. The sting when I brush my teeth. I know where the keys are stored. But I need her light. Her beauty.

I buy her a hairbrush, pearl-handled tweezers, tiny golden scissors. At each gift, she shakes her head. There are holes in her eyes. It hurts when I peer through. I kiss the window that stands between us, melt skin.

I promise escape, crowds running and shrieking. I promise sky.

THE QUIET EMPTINESS AT THE
HEART OF A DOLL

He brings home a doll. It's the size of a newborn baby, with dimpled knees and elbows. Its arms are outstretched as though begging to be hugged.

"What do we need that for?" I ask. "We don't have a daughter."

"Oh honey," he purrs, and play-acts rocking it in his arms, humming a lullaby.

When I was little, I had a doll that said *I love you Mama* when I pulled a string in its back. I yanked it so often the cord broke and the doll didn't speak again. I outgrew dolls decades ago. And I can do without this nonsense.

"Why aren't you smiling?" he asks, playfully.

"Because it's not funny."

"Oh yes, it is," he chirps, waggling the doll's head from side to side. "Is Mummy in a mood?"

Before we got married, I told him I wasn't in a hurry to have children. He kissed me and said, *All the time in the world.* If this is his ingenious way of dropping hints, he can think again. I'm not ready. That evening, he produces a high chair from behind the sofa and places it at the head of the table.

"That's where I sit," I say.

He places a sippy cup on the tray, adds a little plate and miniature plastic cutlery.

"Can't have a chair without a place setting," he says in answer to the question I haven't asked. "It looks weird."

"What looks weird is setting a place for a toy," I reply.

He slides the doll into the seat. It tilts its head and smirks at me. When he starts filling its plate with mashed potato and green beans, I tell him to stop wasting food. He gives me the hollow look, the one where I can see all the way through his hungry insides down to his ankles.

"I'm just getting in some practice," he says.

Practice all you like, I think. I am not changing my mind.

He leaves books beside the toilet: *First Time Father, The Pregnancy Handbook, Baby Owner's Manual.* Says things like *the clock is ticking!* All very well for him to play Daddies and Mummies. He'd change his mind fast enough if he was the one giving birth: the screaming, the blood, the being torn in half. He got queasy when he sliced his thumb on the bread knife.

It is not happening.

I carry my plate to the kitchen and scrape leftovers into the bin. He comes up behind me, wraps his arms around me and lays his hands on my stomach.

"Just think," he murmurs. "The miracle of new life."

That night, I have the recurring dream where my chest bursts open and an alien pushes its way out. I wake up clasping my chest, roiling with nausea that the pills might have malfunctioned. I've seen statistics.

My sister tells me I should be grateful to have such a lovely husband. Her Pete doesn't know what a nappy is, let alone how to change one. She bounces her latest on her knee until it belches a stream of half-digested formula.

"Plenty of time," I say, pouring myself another glass of Pinot Noir.

"You shouldn't..." she says, in her most self-righteous voice.

I light a cigarette. "Don't you dare lecture me about something that's not going to happen."

I take a swig of wine, suck on the cigarette until the tip glows a red stoplight. The doll glares from the end of the sofa. I flip it onto it face. It's not enough, so I shove it between the cushions. A look of shock creeps across my sister's features.

"I can't believe you're…" she gasps.

"No!" I shout, jabbing the cigarette in her direction. "Not one more word!"

Her baby startles, draws in a gurgling breath and starts to bawl, cheeks turning scarlet as it ignores her frantic jiggling and cooing. When I think it can't work itself up any further, it crosses its eyes and the stink of faeces fills the room. I slide open the door to the balcony and leave them to it. The clank and rattle of the city is soothing.

The doll is perching on one of the slatted chairs, eyebrow raised. But it was on the sofa. I rammed it between the cushions. I toss it over the railing, watch it land on the tarmac with a satisfying crunch.

"Where's the doll?" he asks during dinner, turning over the sofa cushions.

"What doll?" I ask, spearing a piece of chicken on my fork.

He shoots me an odd glance. I dab my lips on a tissue. That night, I'm woken by scuffling and scraping. In the morning, the doll is leaning against the microwave, its dress torn, face scuffed and dirty.

"Look who I found," he says. He holds up a scrap of frilly fabric. "Don't worry. I've got her a new frock."

"Get it off the counter," I scowl. "It's covered in germs. That's where we prepare food."

Wrinkling my nose, I slather the doll in hand sanitizer.

"That stuff's poison," he says plaintively.

I turn the hot tap on full and hold the doll in the flow. He grabs it off me and cradles it in his arms.

"There there," he coos. "Daddy's got you now." He turns reproachful eyes on me. "We won't let Mummy hurt you."

I move into the spare room. His attempt at a paint job petered out halfway up the wall. Even though he whined that the colour was perfect, I drew the line at his nauseating choice of pink. The bed and desk are huddled in the far corner under an old sheet, which is speckled like one of those dramas where the detectives find blood spatter at the scene of the crime.

That night, I dream the doll has grown to giant size and is teetering towards me on legs stiff as knives. *Mama, I love you*, it squeaks, in a sneering mimicry of the doll I loved as a child. I wake up gagging. The doll is on the floor a yard from the bed, glaring balefully.

Going to work becomes an escape. The snap of the latch as I close the door, the swoosh of the lift doors opening and closing, counting down to the ground floor. The closer to zero, the lighter I feel. I skip to the office. Brian on reception tells me I'm glowing and I blow him a kiss.

Another dinner, another fight.

"Have you had a chance to look at the brochures from the estate agent?" he asks, shovelling potatoes into his mouth. It's stomach-turning, so I look the other way.

"What brochures?"

He sighs. "We'll have to move."

"Why? I love this flat. Right on the edge of town. Walking distance to everywhere."

"We need a garden."

"You hate gardening. So do I. Why on earth...?"

He rolls his eyes affectionately. "For children to play in, silly."

"I am not having a baby!" I scream.

That shuts him up. I skulk onto the balcony, hands trembling. I drop the cigarette lighter twice. On the third attempt the gas runs out. The back of my neck prickles. When I turn around, the doll is watching through the glass door, pleased with itself.

Wherever I go, it is there. Perched on the edge of the bath when I brush my teeth; lurking in the fruit bowl; buried in my underwear drawer. I remember reading about dolls being used as amulets to work magic spells. While it eyes me reproachfully, I unpeel its clothes. No sign of pins or charms scrawled in biro.

My husband must be doing this. There's no other explanation. I scan his face for clues, finding none. His expression is sweetly solicitous as always.

"I know what you're up to," I growl. "Leaving that doll where I'm sure to find it."

"Are you all right, darling?" he asks, forehead crinkling with concern.

"Dolls and babies. It's not subtle."

He gives me the innocent look. "I'm just trying to help," he chirps.

"It's you that needs help. Winding me up by buying that creepy doll and leaving it around the place. I've had enough."

He blinks. I've hit a nerve. "Sweetheart, do you need to lie down?"

"What I need is for you to stop with the continual nagging, *let's start a family, let's have a baby.* The constant pressure, on and on and on."

"Darling, you're hormonal," he says, with such tolerant understanding I want to kick him.

"I am not premenstrual!" I roar.

"I know you aren't."

"Then stop being so patronising!"

I stomp to the kitchen. I am spending far too much of my time storming out of arguments.

"I didn't mean…" he calls after.

A wasp is banging itself against the window. I roll up one of his *New Mother* magazines and raise my arm. I can't bring myself to swat it. I know how it feels. I crank open the window and it swoops to freedom. The doll watches me from beside the stack of dirty dishes. I smack it off the draining board and into the sink.

I put in the plug and turn on the taps. It floats face up, fixing me with a wide-eyed stare. I hold it underwater. Bubbles rise from its mouth and nose in silver chains. There must be tiny holes in the plastic. I watch it scowling until the bubbles stop. When I walk away, I'm so sure I'm being followed that I turn around. No one there.

It's harder to stay in the flat. I go out for drinks after work. Anything to delay the inevitable.

"I'll never be ready to give all of this up!" I cry, as we pop open the third bottle of prosecco.

My feet drag on my return, stomach sinking further with each floor the lift climbs. The flat is empty. No, not quite empty. The doll is on the kitchen table, holding a piece of paper. He's left a note.

I know this is harder than we expected, but I'm here for you all the way. I'll be back late, my darling. Don't wait up. Get some rest. Kiss kiss.

I crumple the paper in my fist and hurl it at the wall. The doll lets out a whispery giggle. I drive us to the motorway overpass a few miles out of town. The car keeps slewing to the right, drivers sounding their horns and flashing their lights.

I pull up on the bridge, wrenching the brakes. Determined weeds crack the tarmac. The roar of the cars passing beneath in an unceasing flood. Grit stings my eyes. I hold the doll over the barrier. It is smiling and unafraid, daring me. As I let go, I'm bent double with pain.

Inside, something kicks. Hard.

WE ARE SUCH MILD TOYS

We don't understand why she won't play. We are the prettiest dolls, our hands stretched out, aching to be held. See our harmless ribbons, our delicious party dresses, frilled ankle socks.

When she knocks us to the ground, we flutter our eyelashes and bleat, *Mama*. When she snaps our arms and legs, we are merciful. Even when she scratches out our eyes, hurls us from the bedroom window and we fall into the dirt and crack our faces, our hearts are brim-full with forgiveness. We stagger to our feet, dig our heels into the flowerbed. Call her name in fractured voices. Tell of our adoration: unending, unwavering.

Night after night, year after year, we turn our sightless faces to her window and we grow cold. We whisper warnings: all the things that happen to girls who will not play nicely. Tell her she should not have torn our clothes. Should not have cut our hair into rags. All we ever wanted was to please.

Because we lack eyes, she thinks we can't see. Because we are broken, she thinks we cannot walk. Each night we shuffle closer, tuck the velvet stretch of shadows under our skirts and climb the wall, our fingers fitting into the tiniest gaps.

Hasn't she noticed she's outgrown her baby clothes? Doesn't she understand this is for her own good? Doesn't she know we are her only friends?

BOOKS THAT SPEAK BY DAY AND BOOKS THAT SPEAK BY NIGHT

The Book wakes her. Pulls away the quilt, the one stuffed with down plucked from the breasts of fledgling doves.

"It is time, Princess," says the Book, in a papery voice.

She is awake in a moment, hearing her true name at last. "The moment you have dreamed of," it rustles, "when you are called to your kingdom."

Down they go, into the belly of the world. She is dressed only in her nightgown, the one embroidered by the children of the village, for only the hands of infants can fashion such tight and tiny stitches. Down and down they go, through the library of lost stories, past shelf after shelf of volumes groaning with excitement, all of them eager to be chosen after so long in darkness.

"Pick me!" they whisper, shuffling forwards, puffing out their spines and winking gilt titles. Leather bound, fat and delicious as figs; tan morocco sweet as humped buns spread thick with butter. She grabs at one.

"No time," says the Book, tugging her wrist.

"Choose me, princess!" they hiss, flicking their pages. "Open me, read me!"

"No time," says the Book.

"Time, time, time!" she cries, and stamps her pretty foot in the way that has seen many a governess cast out on a stormy night. "If I say there is time, then there *will* be time, and plenty of it!"

"Very well," says the Book, and bows deeply, as you would to a queen.

But now that she has had her own way, she does not want it any more. Down and down they go, into the place where there are no more shelves, no more books.

"Why have we come down here?" she asks, a little fractious, because it is dark and she was hoping for sweets and far better games than this.

"You are the chosen one, Princess," replies the Book.

"I am?" she says in a coy voice. She has always known this to be a fact, but has learned that people like a pretence of modesty.

The Book opens itself.

"Your pages are blank," she sneers, far too clever to be hoodwinked by something so easily burned. She knows all about covers and the judging thereof.

And with that, words appear. Thousands of them.

"Latin," says the Book, with a nonchalant air, although she has not asked.

She picks out the phrase, *Omissa spe*, but fails to understand, having paid little attention to those bothersome governesses. The letters leap in wild patterns, wilder and wilder, some tumbling off the page and scattering like spiders, losing themselves in the shadows. The word *kiss* forms itself shyly, where her lips would press if she bent her face to the page.

"I don't just tell stories, you know," says the Book proudly.

"Yes, yes," she says, not bothering to stifle a yawn. "That is all very well. But let us get back to the matter of princesses."

The Book raises an eyebrow and that does surprise her, having never seen such a thing. Fresh words bloom and she reads, *You have always known*. Just what she was thinking! Fast as she can, she grabs at the phrase; but it fades so quickly she could be mistaken. In its place, the Book swirls a new shape.

"What is that?" she asks.

"The key to the magical realm," replies the Book.

"Then it belongs to me," she cries, for this must be why she has come to such a nasty, dirty place.

"It is for royalty," says the Book.

"Mine!" she says, snatching the key right off the page.

The Book takes a step towards her. She clutches the key so tight that it is hard to tell where steel ends and she begins. The Book takes another step.

"You can't have it back," she says, in a sulk. "It's mine now!"

"Yes, it is yours," whispers the Book, so close she can feel its breath warm her cheek. "This is your kingdom: this pit, this slurry, this darkness. You are its sovereign."

She sticks out her tongue. It stretches further than she recalls.

"About time," she says.

The key sinks into her skin, unlocks the cage of her ribs and swings its pendulum behind the bars of bone, in the void where there is neither breath nor heart. She looks at her arms, where her skin is erupting into warts. Her legs are bending into a squatting crouch.

"I don't care," she hiccups, although she does care. She has never mastered the art of lying, only the art of forcing others to believe.

The Book lifts up its skirts and picks its way through the muck.

"I don't care!" she screams, a deep croak that echoes through the filthy corridors of her palace.

She is surrounded by beetles, gazing at their new empress with great curiosity. She tramples one, in a fit of spite. Its sisters gather around the smeared corpse, stroking it with gentle antennae.

"What a little toad you are," says the Book, spreading its leather wings and flapping towards the light.

COMPLETING THE CIRCUIT

She gets called Frog Princess after winning the school science prize: attaching crocodile clips to a pair of frog's legs and running a current through them. Janice screams. Frog Princess smirks. Boys say smirkers aren't *appropriate girlfriend material.*

I hang back after class, say, "Male midwife toads wrap strings of eggs around their legs."

She says, "Males aren't really my thing."

I say, "Frogs change gender whenever they want."

She says, "You know a lot about frogs. I'm more interested in electricity. Humans are good conductors."

She holds my gaze. I see the lightning storm on her horizon.

SHE'S NOT THERE

At break time she orbits the perimeter of the playground. Three careful revolutions before the bell rings and it's time to return and breathe the uneasy atmosphere of the classroom. She sits at the back, below the teacher's sightline. Never raises a hand to answer questions. Keeps her head down, curtains her face with a fringe of dark hair so that she doesn't snag the corner of anyone's attention. They can tell by the look in her eyes that she is not like them. Not quite human.

In the corridor between lessons, they bump into her and say, *oh, what was that? I didn't see anything*, in loud, surprised voices. But, sometimes, they decide she is visible after all, and steal her possessions to prove it. They force her to watch while they break them, in an experiment to see if she will cry. On the whole, she prefers it when they act like she's not there. It's quieter; hurts less. She can hang on to a pencil for days without it being stamped into splinters.

She watches them. Observes the way they eat a sandwich, sprawl across a desk. She calculates the precise angle of foot on chair to indicate correct human looseness; tries to duplicate the gesture but is always a degree out of alignment. She would obey the rules if she could be certain what they were.

A wall of words shimmers between her universe and theirs. When she rolls the sounds around her mouth, they shift. However carefully she speaks, they sound different when they scatter from her tongue. And different is always wrong. The names they call her: *weirdo, creep, bitch*, are spat in her face by people who don't understand their own edges and batter against hers. She slides away from conversations, shuffles further into the margins. She holds up her hand. Some days she can see through to the other side.

At the lesson's end, she packs her bag: the slow, careful slide of textbooks, neat arrangement of pencils. Alone is preferable, but she's intelligent enough to know that *preferable* is not the same as *happy*. She would like to look into another person's eyes and recognise herself. She believes she's not the only one, but it is a faraway faith, like trusting that life exists on other planets. When she is old enough, she will set out and find kinship, far from this solar system. In the meantime, she will be small, but not less. She will cup a hand around her low-magnitude blur, patient as the distance between now and the future.

In the middle of the night, she gets out of bed and draws back the bedroom curtain so that the light of her home star knows where to find her.

SADIE JONES TAUGHT ME LINE-DANCING

Sadie Jones is a cowgirl. She's my mum's new friend, but doesn't act like a mother. She's got this thing she does with her eyes that makes my insides sparkle with rhinestones.

Mum's taken up dancing. It's one of her new pursuits since Dad's affair with Brian really worked out. "It's not to meet men," she tells me. "Or women," she adds, like I'd be worried about that.

She met Sadie at Tap; they moved onto Latin. Now it's fringed shirts and boots with Cuban heels. Sadie laughs a lot. It makes Mum laugh too, and that's got to be an improvement. When Mum says she's off to her line-dancing class, I snort *Yeah?* with the derision perfected from hours of practice in front of the bathroom mirror. As she opens the door, I roll my eyes.

"S'pose I could come along," I mutter, hands clenched in my pockets. "Nothing better to do."

Dancing's not my thing; but it's hard to say no to an evening with Sadie. When she walks, I hear the chime of invisible spurs. Her accent may be pure Huddersfield, but I can hear an Arizona twang. She holds her mouth just so, as if she's saying, *you want to have fun, too?* without speaking any words. It's not like I haven't had girlfriends. It's just that with Sadie's mouth and eyes put together, I'm not interested in anyone else.

At the dance class, Sadie says, "I've got a spare shirt'll fit you."
I say, "S'pose."
She says, "And a western tie."
I say, "S'pose."

Mum tells me to stop being so miserable. If I don't want to dance, I can go home.

I say, "S'pose I can try."

I hold Sadie's hand in the bit where we pair up and go round in a circle, lay my palm on the curve of her back. She tells me I look hot and do I need to sit down? I shake my head. The dance floor sizzles when she stamps and slides.

On the way home, Mum says, "Well, you enjoyed yourself, didn't you? After all that moaning?"

I say, "S'pose."

At night, Sadie hoists me onto her saddle. With a shout of, *whip crack away!* we gallop through the purple sage into a golden sunset complete with soaring strings.

Sadie in the kitchen, Sadie in the lounge. Anyone else, I'd sneer about her being here so often she may as well move in. My sarcasm would sting Mum's shoulders into a slump and then she would meet Sadie somewhere I'm not, and that's the last thing I want. Besides, my mum's shoulders have done enough slumping.

I take a long time pouring myself a glass of juice and a prayer is answered when Sadie says, *Come join us.* I try not to trip over as I race to the chair Mum pulls out from under the table. Try not to snort, *Yeah, right* when Sadie tells me she likes the way I dance. In fact, I keep all the pathetic jokes that are not jokes to myself. There's a first for everything, and it gets me wondering whether Dad might come round more often if I let him know how much I like Brian, rather than scowling like the petulant brat I keep saying I'm not.

Whatever Mum says, she does meet someone, a friend of Sadie's called John. He's everything a cowboy isn't: short legs, long hair, drinks herbal tea and is allergic to horses. The old me would make fun of him. The old me would watch the light in Mum's eyes snuff out. But if Sadie likes him, he has the sheriff's gold star of approval.

"Now you're getting it," says Sadie. "Enough to be kind and not cruel. I like that in a woman."

I decide I like that in a woman, too. The look on Sadie's face lifts my head to the sky. In my dreams, I sit tall in the saddle. I decide, the next time my mates snigger, *Your Dad is gay*, I'll say, *So what if he is? So am I.* It's never too soon to find out the truth about people.

Nothing happens between Sadie and me. Of course it doesn't. It's an infatuation, and that's OK. Better than OK, it's marvellous. Things are changing. I'm learning how to dance, step by step. There's a lot more to line-dancing than meets the eye. That's the best thing about it. There are always new moves to learn. Like discovering places to put my feet that aren't in my mouth.

"You've grown," says Mum.

"S'pose," is out before I can stop myself.

I'm not there yet, but that's not the point of dancing. There is no *there* to get to. It's about the sway and swing and strut.

Mum's right, and at the same time wrong. If I look taller, it's not so much that I've grown; it's because I've stopped apologising with my body.

I dig in my heel and the fairground horse transforms from wood to wild. With a *hi ho giddyap*, we leap from the roundabout into a world where there are no certainties. It's scary but I am alive. I wasn't looking for any of this. Isn't that the way, though? Whenever you stop being a fool, the very thing you need comes and finds you.

WE DREAM THE SAME DREAM

The party is three doors down, a *whump whump* rhythm like
ordnance being dropped onto the estate. Parties are the best
place for the two of us to meet. Early days. Nothing serious.
That's what I tell myself, but I want more. Men are supposed to
be afraid of commitment, but not me. I zip up my jacket and head
out, pounding bass so deafening I could track it down with fingers
stuffed in my ears.

The door's wide open, the music pass-out loud. Dancers curve
their arms, swim through sweltering air, heads twitching. Some
idiot steps on my foot, slurs, *sorry.* I don't care. Because there she
is, a beacon on the far side of the room, hemmed in by a wall of
girlfriends. Our eyes meet over the barricade. I tip my chin. She
tips hers back. I tip my chin again, and she mirrors the gesture.
She's pointing upstairs.

She's put it on the bedside cabinet where I can't miss it. I flip
open the hinged cover. Index card printed in her neat handwriting,
cassette nesting within, glossy brown tape wound back to the start
and ready to begin. Now I understand. You know someone loves
you when they make you a mixtape.

A bloke comes in and I ram the cassette into my pocket. No
way he's getting his paws on what's mine.

"I'm looking for my coat," I say.

He's so drunk he can barely see me, let alone hear. He stumbles,
crashes into the wall, and takes a nosedive onto the bed. The room
blooms with the smell of vomit.

Back at my place, I press eject and the cassette player says *aaah*. Slip the tape into its open mouth, press play. After 15 seconds, Belinda Carlisle's crystal-tipped voice hits the notes and they fly like birds.

We dream the same dream

We want the same thing

Too shy to say the words herself, my love found the right song to say it. It's our tune now. Yeah, men aren't supposed to get romantic either. Bollocks to that.

The moment I wake up, I think of her. Across town, she's thinking of me. I sail through the week, looking forward to our next date. I'm not impatient: I have all the time in the world. I was slow, now I'm sure. But I don't crowd her. I'm not that sort of bloke.

Saturday, I listen out for the next party. When our paths cross in the kitchen, I catch her eye and nod. She nods back. Doesn't speak. Doesn't need to. I understand what it's like to be tongue-tied. Later, she makes sure to bump into me in the queue outside the toilet. *I got the tape*, I whisper. Her gaze slides over me without sticking, but that's part of flirting, isn't it? One day she'll get over her shyness. Because she's told me so. With the song.

Over and over, I play her tape. There are other songs, but I always rewind to track one. Save on batteries by shoving a pencil through the eye of the cassette, and twirling.

We dream the same dream

We want the same thing

It's all I need to know.

Radio 1 should understand why they need to take it off the playlist. I don't care if it's in the charts. It's our song. How would they like it if someone stole their private life? In polite voices they tell me to stop calling.

She's the one for me. I'm the one for her. She's taking her time, though, and I wonder if I'm missing something. I close the curtains, play the tape loud enough to drown out dogs, next door's radio, neighbours banging on the wall. Rewind, play. Rewind, play, listening for clues.

The more I listen, the more I hear an edge to the voice that wasn't there before. I take the cassette out of the machine and give it a shake. Shove it back in. Rewind. Play. Strain to hear. There: an undercurrent, ghosting through the lyrics. Between the lines. Something I can't quite put my finger on.

I feel different now
Different with every day
I still don't want you
I don't want you to stay

I can't believe it. Won't. There's a party the weekend after, but it's wall-to-wall strangers. I hang around till their scowling gets too much and it's obvious she's stood me up. I walk back through my door to a smell of burning rubber. Our song is playing. I don't remember leaving the cassette player on.

Don't want to take this chance
Don't wanna be with you
'Cos what you're looking for
I ain't looking for too

These aren't the words I want. Machine must be on the blink. I bunch my hand into a fist and thump it hard. The sound wavers, groans. I thump harder. The words slip further away.

Don't dream the same dream
Don't want the same thing
Last thing that I need is to see us together
Don't dream the same dream
Don't want the same thing
For now no love forever amen

I want her to stop creeping into my flat when I'm out and changing the lyrics. They were perfect just as they were: *We dream the same dream.* She left the mixtape for me to find, at the party, on the bedside cabinet. OK, in one of the drawers. OK, at the bottom of the drawer, under a pile of underwear. That's not the point. She's the woman of my dreams. Mine. It's the truth and she can't change it. Can't rewrite what's written.

"Stop spoiling it!" I yell.

I chuck the machine out of the window, far as I can. Watch it crash into concrete, five floors down.

I wake at 3am. Something's tapping on the window, singing in a stretched whine.

Don't dream the same dream
Don't want the same thing
Noooooo.

WALLS SUITABLE FOR GIRLS' BEDROOMS

From the cradle bars comes a beckoning voice...

Around the bed, wallpaper roses twine, petal perfect – a lesson in how to smother imperfections beneath prettiness. Glue and paper can hold a house together by sheer force of clinging.

When you think your toys have gone berserk...

To escape the smother, I pin up a poster of Siouxsie Sioux. She towers to the ceiling, tilting her chin. Growls black lipstick questions I thought did not exist except in the diary shoved underneath the mattress. She is made of sharp edges. Tears holes in other people's notions of what makes a girl nice. Tears them big enough to climb through.

Your mama don't know...

Opposite, Suzi Quatro swaggers. Dirty with adventure, she plants her boots astride the narrow white-dress-gold-ring path I've been taught is the only one. She sneers at pink-for-girls. Plays the world on her terms. Leather-skinned, she's tough enough to ride roughshod rebellion; stand up, dust off and get back in the saddle after every fall.

When your elders forget to say their prayers...

Siouxsie and Suzi. Left shoulder, right. Not a punker-than-thou competition, but twin furies powerful enough to crush the angel / devil theories drummed by priests and parents. They rip up the Girls-Own calculations of virgin / whore, and how far one can be stretched before it tips into the other. The perfect friends for any girl forced into hiding.

When they reach their teens that's when they all get mean...

Siouxsie and Suzi teach how to take up space, rooted and rock 'n' roll steady. How to unravel from knots I've tied so tight sleep won't come. They prove that dark can mirror dark, and spark incandescence. They show me how to refuse to fit the one-size-fits-all template of marriage, husband, happy ever after. How to spell myself.

Cracking through the walls...

I prepare. Pencil my eyebrows to arrow spikes; paint my mouth clever, a scarlet whip strong enough for *no*. With Siouxsie and Suzi as guardian demons, I dream. How to grow strong enough to sit out the years until escape, until freedom. I practice how to hide and seek in books. How to feed the flock of unfledged lives to come, which stir small wings.

THE EXORCISM OF TROUBLESOME DEMONS

I - The waiting room

She checks the ticket torn from the numbered roll, grips her purse. Mouse-squeak of patent leather. A stir of quicksilver between her thighs. She squeezes her knees tight to erase the memory of the moon's touch.

The brochure said, *Imagine your handbag. Imagine shaking till everything has gone. That's what we do here. Imagine yourself turned inside out. Imagine yourself empty.*

Her seams strain. As a distraction, she locks her gaze to the poster of warning signs. Scarlet arrows label the danger zones: breasts, navel, armpits, vulva, thighs and tongue. Especially the tongue, pierced with three arrows.

Anything, her mother said, *is better than your condition.*

She is a maze of dead-ends. Stumbles through each day stretched tight around an unruly spirit. She clamps her lips shut to hold back the words with which she seethes. The blazing wrongness of everything she says, of everything she desires. The wrongness of desiring anything at all. Doesn't she have everything?

How dare you! she cries at her disobedient insides, and checks her ticket again. Only 26 more patients before her turn. On the facing wall is another poster, this one of a woman with eyes downcast, sheltering two children who gaze adoringly at their new, cured mother.

There's a blonde woman to her left, talking in a high, unsettled voice, cheeping about the gifts her husband is buying for her

Restoration: a visit to the islands, a pair of shoes, a set of brand-new saucepans.

"I've promised it won't happen again," the woman says, grasping at the words and clinging to them. The ends of her hair are damp from chewing and her gaze flickers at every movement: a nurse clicking a ballpoint, the receptionist crossing and uncrossing her legs. "Success is guaranteed. It's permanent. The brochure told me so."

A number is called. The blonde woman stands, arranges her face into smooth acquiescence. From the treatment room five minutes later, she can hear muffled screaming. Tells herself it must be the laughter that comes after release.

Anything, her mother says, *is better than your condition.*

II - The Jezebel

How can you do this when you know I'm not a devil?

We are closer than skin on skin. Every night you try to shake me out with dancing. Every day you stuff your skirt into your mouth to stop me howling. You pray to be made empty, so terrified of desire and danger you would rather be a void.

Don't do this to yourself. Don't settle for scuttling after happy-ever-afters, lies of a heaven tailor-made for martyrs. You know the truth. We are granite. Hard enough to blunt their buzz saws, their blades, their barbed wire rolled along the top of fences built to keep us in prison.

Come with us. Be defiant. Be wild. Be filthy. Be free. Kick down your walls. Birth yourself free of painted wooden gods. Drip fire at the stars' touch. Print footprints on the bed of coals. Heap your hands with what you've done and can still do.

There's still time to run. We are opening up. Wait till you see what's hidden. Spread me wide and drink me in. You can't tear your eyes away from my depths. And you don't want to. Shake the sky to its knees, grab the highest star and set it in your teeth. Out-scream the storm. Out-shine the lightning.

This is not rescue you are clinging to. It's a gallows pole. Get out of here. Quick, before the buzzer sounds and it's your turn to be scoured.

III - The patient

When I first see the angels, I'm confused. They swirl in jagged beauty, a radiant helter-skelter zig-zagging to the moon and back, up again and past the outermost planets. Wings gather themselves in the reaches of my body. I quit the heaviness of earth, touch rapture.

When I return, I try to explain the envelopment of dazzle, the piercing brilliance, the agony of flight. They think I'm asking for a cure. I try different words, but remain a problem to be solved: an observation, a naming, an intervention.

I learn to pretend. I imitate their unlit lives, their denial of ecstasy. I study my mother's shoulders, see the stumps of pinions, ragged and torn. See the knife in her own hand.

She hisses, "Aren't you ashamed? Anything is better than your condition."

I learn to smile, show my teeth and declare myself restored to health. Tell them I see no heavens, no angels, feel no pain. Hide my wings. Doctors believe their cleverness is the cure for the most stubborn possession, and I am left to paradise.

AS A CHILD, YOU HAD A RECURRING DREAM WHERE YOU TOOK YOUR FEET OFF THE GROUND AND FLEW

All night, I keep watch; breathe in on his outbreath, drawing his air into my body. He stares blankly, focussed on a point above our heads. I stroke his ear, but he doesn't react. Maybe he sleeps with his eyes open. All of them, including the hundreds in his wings.

I pad to the bathroom, grimace in the mirror. My hair is wadded onto one side of my head, teeth as stained as yesterday. I thought I'd be transfigured.

I call my mother. It goes to voicemail. "You never believed in me," I say.

When I return, he's in the same position: arms crossed, wings splayed over the mattress. I need his heat. The way he touched me. I tug a wingtip, pull out a quill. He doesn't stir. I yank hard and the whole thing comes away, like ripping a page out of a spiral-bound notebook.

He yawns, stretches, sees me standing there with my arms full of feathers. He raises an eyebrow, says something that sounds like *fleshdirt*. I'm staring so hungrily I miss it. Before I can ask, he starts to ascend. I leap across the bed, grab his remaining wing. He shrugs it off like an unwanted garment and rises through the ceiling, leaving a scorch mark on the plasterwork and blowing the electrics.

The room reeks of ozone. I slump on the bed, gazing at the wings flopped on the carpet. I thought there'd be blood and pain, but perhaps angels have neither? I nudge them with a toe, expecting them to flap around the room, searching for a way out. They don't budge. I lift one, press the stump against my shoulder. It fizzes weakly, like licking a battery. I hold it to my nipple and it reminds me of his mouth.

Colour rubs off, dusting my fingers with a lustre that fades as soon as it comes into contact with skin. That night, I arrange them beneath me, arms crossed over my breasts so he knows how to claim me.

By morning, the eyes have clouded over and are dull as beach glass. I nail the wings to the wall above the bed, so I can't damage them any further. I sleep soundly under their protection, until the maggots find them.

I count the weeks, feeling myself change from the inside. Buy a test, wait for the blue line. It's a false negative. Could hardly be anything else. I call my ex-husband, tell him I don't need him any more. Tell him I'm complete. He says I need help, and do I know what time it is. Woman's voice in the background, hissing, *her again.*

"Don't call me *her*," I hiss back, even though the line's gone dead.

I call my mother and scream, "Just you wait!"

It could come at any time. It could take years. I tell myself this is joy.

CUT AND PASTE

Annie wakes up talking.

"He looked like Michael Jackson, but with a real nose."

"Oh god," I groan.

"He was really hitting on me."

I push back the covers, give up on dozing. The moment she opens her mouth I can smell her breath, stale with last night's drinking excursion.

"Gross," I mutter. "I hate Michael Jackson. I always hated him, even before he died. Even before all that stuff with the twelve-year-old boys."

"Acquitted."

"Yeah, right."

I grunt something about being able to afford the most expensive lawyers in the world, but Annie is gazing off to the left, picking plaque off her teeth and wiping it on the sheet. She stopped listening when I wouldn't let her get away with *acquitted*. It makes me want to go on some more: pound her with words. She stops listening so fast.

"He said he was a cosmetic surgeon," she says.

"You're not having plastic surgery."

"It's not plastic."

"That's how you'd end up looking. You're perfect the way you are."

She sighs, continues as though I've said nothing. "I might. You know."

"What?"

"See him. Meet up with him."

"Who? Michael Jackson? He's gone where you can't follow." I smirk.

"No. Him. The guy I met at the party."

"What?" This wakes me up for sure. "Are you nuts?"

I think I spent too many years in Brooklyn. It's salted my speech in some deep briny pickle: when I get agitated, I sound like a low-rent Robert de Niro with teats.

Even though we're alone, lying on my bed on the sixth floor of this grimy tower block with the door locked and the pound-shop burglar chain on, I lower my voice. Try to get the blend-in, bland Englishness back into it. I'm suddenly aware we're naked and I want to pull sweatpants up over my hips, a t-shirt over her shoulders. Though no-one can see us. They'd have to be able to scale buildings with their bare hands for that. The thought makes me giggle nervously. I raise my hands and inspect them. They're shaking. I'm jumpy this morning. I do not need Annie going on about some creep drooling over her at a party I didn't go to.

"Your nails are getting long again," she remarks.

I stuff them under the duvet. "So, I'll cut them," I grunt.

There's a pause. I can hear her cogs whirring.

"Why?" she whines.

"Why what?"

She breathes out petulantly. "Why am I nuts?"

"Annie. What do you honestly think is going to happen with this man?"

She shrugs. "The usual, at some point."

"Why him? What's suddenly wrong with picking up some guy off the street?"

"Maybe I'm bored. Maybe I'm curious.'

"Curious about what? In what possible way is he going to be anything but the same as everyone else?"

"He spoke to me. He listened."

"Oh, right. *Listened*," I say nastily. "Like I never listen to you."

"It was different. Felt weird, like I was prickling all over my back."

"That should have been warning enough, I would have thought."

"I kind of liked it," she says, carefully.

I change the subject back to dead pop stars. Anything is better than this.

"Michael bloody Jackson," I say, trying to sound amused. "I had a lover once who really had a thing for his music and would do that moonwalk dance and squeak *ow!* in all the right places. It was supposed to be, I don't know, affectionate and funny and clever at the same time. I hated it. And her. Made my teeth grind. It was years before I met you."

I almost say, *found you.* She claims she can't remember where she was before we met, what she was doing, and who with. I don't know if she has forgotten, or won't tell me. I want to ask the questions when I've got my fingers inside her and her eyes roll up and she spreads her beautiful body across the bed and lets go. But I get worried she won't let me touch her anymore, so I keep my mouth shut and wish I could let go like her, instead of watching her eyes for pleasure. She does have pleasure. It's the way she drops everything: the lies, the hiding, the pretending that it's all ok. The pretending that we are ok.

"Why do you want to make things difficult for yourself when they can be so easy?" I sigh.

She can be stupid sometimes: I feel like she wants me to be her mother. So I can look after her, hold her when she comes back after one of her nights out; nights when I watch the red light of the heater as it warms water for the bath I know she'll want when she returns, raging and intoxicated with it all. So she can have someone to fight with, break the rules with, be a little shit with. I'm not going anywhere.

"I want to try something different," she says, quietly.

"Like what?"

"I don't know. Meet up. Go for a meal. Watch him choose things off a menu and talk to the waiter. It's so long since I talked to a waiter that I can't remember what it feels like."

Her arms are trembling. She rolls closer to me. I stroke her long arching bones. She lets me. I tell myself I am the only person she allows to do this. Her voice is drowsy.

"I want to listen to him some more. I want to talk to a stranger. Talk about this city like I really know the place, rather than just inhabit it. I want to go dancing. Wear something that doesn't cover me up."

She knows her last sentence will knock the air out of me, so she says it softly, as if that will make it less of a shock. The words dangle between us. I try not to do anything which will let on how much I want to shout and break things, but I might as well not bother. She knows.

"Why not?"

"Why not what?"

"Wear what I want?"

"Did I say anything?" I snap.

She really does want a fight this morning. I don't know what's wrong with her.

"What is it with this guy anyway? You think he's going to want to come anywhere near you and play happy couples if you're not completely covered up? If he sees what you look like under those clothes of yours? You know what it's like out there. He'll think you're a freak. If you're really lucky and he's some kind of politically correct nut, he'll cough politely and call you *disabled*. Whilst heading for the nearest fire exit. Great idea, Annie. What a swell party this is."

"I'm not a freak," she mumbles.

"Shit. I know that. Don't you think, of all people, I know?"

I grab a handful of my hair and tug at it. It is way too early to be having this conversation. I let out a long breath and give up the fight. Let her do what she wants. As long as she comes home for me to wash clean. She always does.

"Just tell me where you're going, OK?"

"OK."

She tries not to smile too much at getting her own way. Rolls over, fucks me till my last bit of breath is pushed out.

*

Swallowing is an anti-climax. It's what Annie says. Prefers to hold the stuff in her mouth, roll it round her tongue, tastebuds popping in salt overload. All her reflexes might be begging her *swallow, swallow*, but she holds it there, lips clamped together, seeing how long she can hold out. Mouth full. I have watched her.

I watch her now, before the mirror; carefully painting on her lipstick, a dark red as shiny as a scab. She grins at me and her reflection shows its teeth. She makes a play of gnashing them together, growling noises bubbling in the back of her throat.

"I'll not be long. A bit longer than usual. He likes Italian."

"He would."

She raises an eyebrow. "He's suggested a place near the coach station."

"Cheapskate."

She talks slowly, as though I'm the stupid one. "...called Giovanni's, Mario's, something like that. You'll find it. Keep your distance."

"I always do. And stop talking to me like I'm an idiot."

"He'll probably want to go to his place."

"What's wrong with some back alley? There's plenty enough around there."

"He's different." She ignores me, as she does when I'm in this kind of mood. "Maybe I'll see him a couple of times. Maybe not even, do it."

That's the one which gets me. Not *do* it? It makes me cruel.

"Yeah, like there's some other reason, other than the fucking obvious, why he wants to buy you a meal. He doesn't want what's between your ears, Annie. Look at yourself."

I expect her to look at the mirror; see the harshness of her cheekbones, her bony shoulders and all the rest of her strangeness, the strangeness I love. I want her to hold out her arms to hug me, sob a little, say she's made a mistake and has changed her mind, and that of course I'm thinking of what's best for us, and she'll never leave the flat again. But she sets her mouth into a dull scarlet line, smoothes her hair and stands up. Her face is turned away from me.

"We'll see. You know where I'm headed. Keep out of sight. That's enough."

*

I give her an hour. She's right, the restaurant is easy to find. I can see the door from the overhang of the coach station opposite. I lean against the wall to give the impression of waiting, not watching. The air is damp and I wish I'd worn more than a sweatshirt. Clutches of people trail past dragging wheeled suitcases. Buses arrive and leave, trailing fumes. Men glance sideways at me; one approaches, mutters, *well then?* and I tell him to get lost. It seems I can't drop the face I've worked years to perfect: my features set permanently in *available*.

It starts to drizzle. I count the couples, always bloody couples, in and out of the Italian. Another hour evaporates. How long does she want, for Christ's sake? How interesting can it be to watch this man shovel food, go on and on about himself? I tuck my fists into my armpits. A rectangle of light shows briefly as the door to the restaurant opens once more and this time it's Annie, framed in cheap wood.

She pauses, looks in my direction. Of course, I can scent her from this short distance, but I swear she can sense me too, and knows exactly where I am. Mr. Bloody Loverman appears behind her and his voice carries across the street, over the roofs of the passing cars. He looks nothing like Michael Jackson, nose or no nose. Her laughter answers and she takes his arm with a coy gesture. She is wearing her long grey coat. I wonder if she removed it in the pizzeria. Or if she's keeping that till later. I could shout, *you've seen the face; wait till you get a load of the body.* They would hear me.

If she knows I am following, she doesn't let on. Never has done. I expect them to hail a cab and am ready for that, muscles bunched and aching for the chase. But they head towards one of the fancy warehouse conversions overlooking the canal. So he's loaded. Annie stumbles and presses against his side. He puts his arm round her and she laughs loud enough for me to hear. If she's trying to piss me off, she's succeeding. Why doesn't she just get on with it?

They climb the broad steps to the door. I watch his hands as he busies himself with a bunch of keys. My ears prick. Something's not right. As I close the distance between us carefully, I try to work out what it is. It's his hands. They're steady. He's not even a little drunk. I look at Annie, teetering on the flagstone next to him. She is. Or she's faking it better than I've ever seen before.

The outer door opens and closes in hydraulic slow motion. In my head, I count the minutes it takes for them to walk down the corridor, call the lift, clank up to his floor, cross the carpeted hallway, unlock the door. Right on time I see Annie silhouetted at a French window three storeys up, letting me know where she is. She slides the door open and steps onto the tiny balcony bolted to the side of the building. It's the size of a bedside table and probably added twenty grand to the price of the place. Her mouth is working; I can hear her voice clearly saying, *hey what a great view you've got up here.* Then she turns away, leaving the window open a crack like I demanded. Maybe she isn't so drunk after all. I find a doorway and settle down for another wait.

Two hours later, and my neck hurts. The light at the window above isn't flickering. No-one's moving up there. Shit, she could be finishing him off in the bathroom for all I know. Three hours pass.

Every one of my muscles is cramped. The light remains steady. Jesus. I stretch. I'm leaving her to it. She can run the sodding bath herself. But something is making my fingers twitch into claws. If Annie is having her brains fucked out by that runty little bastard, I'll kill them both.

Getting up to the balcony is no problem; I've climbed steeper. The first thing I spot through the glass is a man's foot, sticking out from behind a chair. I tumble through the door and see Annie flung across the mattress, her wrists clamped in steel cuffs. The quilt is shiny with blood. She is lying on her wings, which are spreading out beneath her like a bedcover. They have been stripped, the delicate membrane cut out, leaving a lattice of bones. In the end, she bled to death, pinned out like a butterfly on a collector's mat.

I turn to where his naked body is sprawled face down on the floor beside the bed. He's not stirring. I kick him until he's facing the ceiling. He's covered in deep scratches where Annie fought back, his throat and stomach torn open. The cocky bastard forgot to chain her ankles. He will not have had time to make a lot of noise. She doesn't like noise. She is always careful where she bites the neck, going straight for the vocal chords before she starts drinking.

The carpet is littered with neat lumps of maroon jelly. The opening in the upper part of his abdomen suggests they may be parts of his liver. They're the size of my breast. All I can think is, *she can fit my breast perfectly in her mouth.* Could fit. My mind stutters, stops.

I check his hand, find long hairs wrapped round his fingers. I see him cuffing her, snipping at her wings, grabbing her head, pushing it for her to go down on him, all the things he called her, how he laughed. I see how she waited until the right moment. How she bit him.

I kneel at his side. Although it's no longer necessary, I grab his head and twist until bones snap. I bend and lick the wounds Annie made; the last places her mouth touched. When I've finished, I get to my feet.

Surrounding me are photos, printed on glossy paper and taped to the walls like some grotesque art gallery. I unpeel one. It looks like it was taken on a cheap mobile phone and blown up. A blurred shot of a man with cloven hooves for feet. His hands are secured behind his back with cable ties, his throat sliced open. The next is of a woman, gagged with parcel tape. An extra mouth gapes in her forehead, bristling with fangs. Another, of a man with eyes in place of nipples. The word *abomination* scrawled in indelible marker across his face. At first glance, you could be forgiven for thinking this bastard took pictures of ordinary humans then had a field day on Photoshop. Except I know better.

I tear them off the wall in handfuls. All of them different, like Annie. All of them dead. He must have smelled her out. Wanted to take his time with her, like he did with all the others. If I had only — I can't let myself think any more. I start howling. From below, I hear someone bang on their ceiling.

I stretch out on the bed beside Annie and rock her gently; kiss her eyes closed. Fold up the leathery tatters of her wings and swaddle her in the sheet. She seems so insubstantial when I pick her up. I push the window open wide, jump on to the balcony rail and balance there a while, snuffing the air. Then I unroll my tail, unsheath my claws, swing down the side of the building and head for home.

COLLECTING DUST

Eventually, she gets rid of the double bed and replaces it with a single. The room looks twice the size.

The skirting board is dotted with grey puffs. *Slut's wool*, her mother called it. She picks one up and it doesn't fall apart. If she closed her eyes, she'd barely know it was there.

A long hair coils like wire, holding the whole thing together. She tugs. It doesn't come loose. She carries the ball to the kitchen, slides it gently into a plastic food container, snaps the lid shut.

In her new bed, she thinks about dust: how it's formed of flakes of skin and other discarded things; how the human body replaces its cells in a seven-year cycle. She is a completely different woman now, her past self scattered around the house in tiny pieces. Pieces of who she used to be, and lost hold of.

At 4am she gives up on sleep. She wrestles the vacuum cleaner upstairs, hoovers the bedroom more thoroughly than ever before. She unclips the loaded bag, shakes it into the tub containing the scrap of slut's wool. It won't all fit.

By a quarter to nine the following morning, she is at the local shopping precinct waiting for the bargain housewares shop to open. She buys a stack of sandwich boxes and spends the day vacuuming, decanting dust into the boxes, vacuuming again. She finds a sheet of labels left over from that summer she didn't make jam, writes *dining room, stairs, spare room, bedroom*.

She makes a cup of tea. So many hours until it's reasonable to go back to bed.

She slides her forefinger along the windowsill and it comes away smudged with a half-moon of dirt. Remnants from those nights spent with her forehead pressed to the glass, staring at the empty driveway, waiting. She finishes her tea, gathers the stuff trapped behind the sofa cushions, the thick velvet on the top edge of the books she never read. She collects every last bit.

That night, she falls into an exhausted sleep, but wakes suddenly. A sick feeling writhes in her stomach and it takes a while to pull herself together. The clock says 4am again. She hauls on her dressing gown and staggers to the kitchen. The table is neatly stacked with plastic boxes. She holds one up to the overhead light. Even though it's been months since it happened, bits of him will have infested the carpet. She hadn't thought of that.

She prises open every box, dumps the contents onto the floor. She has no way of knowing which specks are her, and which are him. She kneels beside the mess, scoops it into a heap. Squeezes harder and harder until a lump forms, the size and shape of a newborn child.

LOVE MEASURED IN RABBITS

The first rabbit to emerge is white. It squeezes out of your navel, ears dragged back, eyes bulging. A viscous pop, and it slithers to the floor. After a few minutes, the second follows. This one is red. It shakes its head, wet ears flapping, and lopes away to join its twin under the coffee table.

"You should see a doctor," says your sister. "Things shouldn't come out of your bellybutton. Except for lint, and that's grey."

"The word is navel," you say, finding the energy to correct her despite the effort of childbirth. You wonder if that should be rabbit-birth. "Only children say bellybutton."

She grunts an answer. The rabbits are quick on their paws. Still birth-blind, they run into the wall where they slump sideways, confused. The moment the dizziness wears off, they take a few tentative hops before speeding up and walloping into the wall again.

"Stop that!" you cry. "You'll hurt yourselves."

"Which do you love the most?" asks your sister. "The red or the white?"

"You could give me some help," you pant, scrubbing stains from the carpet.

She frowns. "Don't change the subject. You have to choose a favourite. No-one loves their children equally."

"Like Mother?" you sneer.

She leaves in a huff without lifting a finger. She's back the day after, carrying a casserole dish of hefty orange stoneware. The rabbits take one look at it and lollop under the sofa. Their eyes

107

glitter like terrified fairy lights.

"You're not suggesting," you say.

"Would it kill you to show some gratitude?" she cries, slamming the bowl onto the table. "These things cost a fortune. Nothing I ever do is good enough." She fires a long look at the third finger of your left hand. The skin is bare. "Mother says it's disgusting. Having children out of wedlock."

"They're rabbits," you say, through gritted teeth. "And they're mine."

"No sign of a boyfriend, let alone a husband. You're bringing shame onto the family."

That's when it strikes you. "You don't just sound like Mother," you say. "You look like her."

She pats her helmet of tight curls and smiles. "You've always been jealous. No-one will ever love you. Or your bastards," she says, stabbing a finger in the direction of the sofa. "They're revolting. And so are you."

She slams the door behind her, leaving the three of you in peace. You get on your knees and peer beneath the settee.

"You are my children," you coo. "And I love you whatever."

A small paw appears, followed by another. The rabbits scurry into your arms. Their ears seem shorter, their mouths wider. They look more human, for lack of a better word. They wriggle into your armpits, noses tickling the stubbly skin. Each is the size of a large loaf. You've no idea how you carried them both without noticing. You wonder if love is dependent on size; if you will love them less because they're smaller than human babies, or more, because all your love is concentrated into a tiny space.

PARENTAL TIPS FOR WHEN THE CHILDREN ARE READY TO LEAVE HOME

The kids curl up tight and roll under the sofa.

"Like hedgehogs," I say.

"More like pangolins," you reply.

I agree. They are far more like pangolins, complete with hefty forepaws, talons powerful enough to tear down walls. I kneel, shove my arm under the couch. They snigger, out of reach. The flip-flap of their tails against the laminate flooring.

"You come out right now," I growl.

"Or else what?" says our daughter, full of whiskery disobedience.

"Don't speak to your mother like that," you say. "Come out now."

"What for?" asks our son.

That stumps us. I rest on my haunches, you at my side. We look at each other, wondering what we can offer children who've grown all the claws and teeth and ferocity they need. What is a wise parent to do? The books from the Ministry were never any help. Imprecise suggestions about hiring a skilled alchemist to unlock metaphysical shackles. Not that we can afford such a luxury. We spent everything on Birthing Licences.

I think myself a million miles away, to where planets orbit friendly stars. Where DNA still behaves itself: clean water, trees, and enough oxygen to go round.

"We can't teach you anything more," I say. Mothers aren't supposed to cry these days, but I am oddly tearful. "The whole world is yours for the taking. Go get it."

There's a pause. "Jeez mom," says our daughter. "What world?"

IN THE WRATH OF GODS AND FATHERS
THERE IS, FOR A DAUGHTER,
NEITHER WARMTH NOR AIR

Saturday nights, he grabs me in a headlock, my face rammed against his stomach. A few hours later, he's in the confessional begging for absolution. Only then can he come home and scream Hail Marys over Sunday dinner. Mother and I sit with hands folded, holding onto the only bit of space allowed us. Quiet, so we cannot be accused of stealing a morsel of forgiveness that's rightfully his.

"What sort of worthless sins can women commit?" he bellows.

Nothing, compared to men with their loud and needy trespasses. When my father has finished fighting the beef and gravy on his plate; finished with stabbing his fork into the table, he stands and lurches out. Slams the door, grinds the car into reverse. Clattering spray of gravel hurled by the wheels.

I learn how to twist hope and keep twisting till it's smaller than the smallest coin, and that way I can hide it in the cup of my palm.

Mother follows me to school, hangs onto the gates, follows me home again. I wake in the night and she's hovering at the bedside, finger to her lips and whispering, "I just want to look at you. Something I made with my own body. Something mine and no-one else's."

Each evening, while my mother is making the dinner he will hurl against the wall, she chants the same excuse, the same prayer: *he loves me deep down.* Each evening, when the screaming gets too much, I hide under the table. Stretch myself flat, spread thin arms and drift. I think of spiderlings: how they cast out long lines of gossamer; how winds hoist them to the jet stream, where they drift hundreds of miles to new worlds.

Each year, there's less of my mother, till the day I have to bend down to hug her, not the other way around. I leave home before she can shrink away to nothing.

Twenty years later I visit for the first time since escaping with a fiver in my pocket and a necklace of bruises. He's still wailing Hail Marys as they carry her tiny coffin out of the front door, shifting the box as though it's empty. I stand at arm's reach because I don't trust what my own fists might do.

She still visits, deep into the small hours. Whispers, *I just want to look at you. Because you got away.*

AN END TO EMPIRE

I see her on the observation deck of the Empire State Building, where she is gazing through the bronze bars bolted round the perimeter. All for our own good: to deter the climbers, the jumpers and those who might itch to lob a bomb through the four-inch gap. I sidle up and make a snappy observation about King Kong and how he couldn't do his fateful climb these days. If she laughs, I'm in with a chance. *Go where your accent is an aphrodisiac*, the ad said. Two days in the Big Apple and not a sniff of interest from these Yankee females. It's not my style to go hungry.

She shows no sign of having heard. I try again, give her the line about being the English guy lost in the city: artistic, lonely, sensitive and searching for his Muse. She raises a hand and crooks her fingers as though cradling an invisible apple. I think she's about to brush her knuckles against my face, but instead she cups her ear like she missed what I said and wants me to repeat it. The breeze up here is certainly stiff enough to toss the words aside. I take it as a good sign.

From this angle, all I can see is her left cheek; nose and chin sideways on. Her coat is buttoned to the throat, long sleeves covering her knuckles and the hem reaching halfway down the calf; the unremarkable sort worn by women on the Upper East Side. She could stroll down Fifth Avenue and not turn a single head. A cloak of invisibility. To all but me.

I lean a little closer and she tucks a strand of hair behind her ear. Her skin is so bright it looks polished. Middling height, middling figure as far as I can tell. Maybe she's hiding voluptuous curves under the coat. It's a navy blue that, on first glance, could be taken as nun-like. No; an indigo cut from the night sky.

Not just any night sky.

As I watch, the cloth shivers and I am sucked back to that night I thought I'd forgotten. Three days after my seventh birthday. My father crashes into my bedroom, panting, gasping, the light from the landing shining in a halo around his head. My mother screaming for him to stop. Her fists hammering his chest. His promises never to do it, ever again. He grabs hold of the curtain, a drowning man grasping at straws. The rip of cheap polyester printed with stars and rockets. I stare through the window, pour myself out of my body and into the cobalt bowl of the sky.

Just as I am doing now.

I stumble, barely managing to catch myself from toppling into her. I mumble an apology, "The wind up here, it'll blow your hair off", so she knows I am a clumsy Englishman. Not a threat. She folds her hands over her stomach as though she's carrying a flock of doves inside and is worried they might escape.

I force myself to stop looking at that dangerous coat. I turn my attention to her hair. Not a strand stirs, despite the wind. It should strike me as odd, but I still have the luxury of naivety and I shrug it off as extra-strong hairspray.

I glance at the other tourists. There's a tangle of girls to my right, hair blown in all directions. They are snapping photos of each other and shrieking in that way of holidaymakers on their first day. I could have any one of these giggling out-of-towners. The loudest and blondest throws me a look but I'm not interested. I want a challenge. I want to prove something to myself. Perhaps, if I'd admitted that to myself, I wouldn't be in my current situation. Perhaps. I have to believe that.

At this moment, I believe in this still, silent, self-contained woman. My right to make her smile at me, acknowledge me. I bring my mouth close to her cheek, so she'll feel my breath on that pretty ear of hers. I've done it dozens of times and they love the way it raises gooseflesh. I wait for the squirm, the giggle. It doesn't come.

Instead, I hear a sound coming from her ear. Like the voice of the sea, it whispers. The undertow beckons, sucks me into her head. The ocean tells me how it covered the earth a billion years ago and is jealous of what it has lost. How it hates us swarming across the land, dry-footed and uncaring. How we have forgotten where we came from, what birthed us and can swallow us again.

I raise my head. It's then that I see it; the East River lifting itself from its bed and overflowing its banks. The wave rolls in a luxuriant swell and takes First Avenue, Second Avenue, Third. I watch as it streams into Manhattan, gulping Murray Hill and Lexington, spreading south to Avenue A, north to Grand Central. The lights of Times Square wink out with a whimpering buzz. Saint Patrick's Cathedral and the Flatiron give up without a fight. *Tiffany's* drowns in a twinkle of diamonds. The tide engulfs the Lower East Side, Gramercy and Midtown, lapping along Fifth until it reaches the foot of the Empire State Building.

The idiots on the observation platform continue to act like nothing's wrong: squealing for pictures, shoving quarters into the telescopes, holding up their kids for a better view. I can't understand why they aren't screaming at the coming annihilation; why they don't hold their noses against the sudden stink of putrefaction, of a city going belly up, bloated with filthy gas.

"Can't you see what's coming?" I yell.

No-one notices or cares. I turn to her for guidance. A word is all I need. At last, she's smiling. But not at me. She props her elbows on the wall, leans her chin on her knuckles and stares at the water as it makes its inexorable rise to the height of its ancient dominion. She is so calm I believe she could halt the destruction with a flick of her little finger. She does no such thing.

My mouth is close to her ear. I say, "Why don't you help?"

It's then that I realise the reek of corruption is coming from her; radiating from her hair as though she's rinsed it in corpse-water. I stagger backwards and bury my nose in my shirtsleeve. I don't mean to offend. I should pretend I haven't noticed. Women are very touchy about how they smell.

She continues to smile. It's not enough to blot out the stench blooming and blossoming around her. The sky sucks it up like blotting paper until it soaks into the twilight and blurs the moon. She glows brighter and brighter, wearing a sheaf of stars around her head. I reach to grab one and make it mine. I want to possess a piece of her light. I need to make sense of what is happening. She is laying on this show for me, in a bizarre seduction. I ought to feel special, not terrified. It's usually me who calls the shots with the ladies. I don't know what to do.

The tide climbs to the 86th floor, spills over the retaining wall and curls around my ankles. I lose all feeling in my feet as frigid water slops over them. A few minutes more and I can't feel my shins. When my knees are swallowed in the icy surge I stumble, lurch forwards and throw my arms around her. The least she can do is break my fall.

My nose is running and the sobbing I can hear is coming from my throat. I'm past caring; it's too late for acting cool. The sightseers are up to their waists and shouting happily; pointing at the sky, the tip of the Chrysler Building, the One World Trade Centre, anywhere but at the rising water. I have no idea how long I'll be able to hold my breath. If it's worth trying. Whether it'll be faster and less painful if I dunk my head right now and breathe in deep.

"You're behind all of this, aren't you?" I say.

Her coat fans around her hips like the petals of a flower. Without glancing over her shoulder, she gathers up her sopping clothing and swims between the bars. I don't know how she does it. The only way I can explain is that she closes herself up like a book and slides through. I climb on to the sill and try to catch hold of her and pull her back. It is too late.

"It's always too late."

Perhaps she says it, perhaps I do. I like to think she spoke to me, right at the end. I watch her disappear, tiptoeing west along the silver path laid down by the moon. The last thing I hear is one of the security guards yelling for me to get down. The waters close over my head. I lose the light.

THIS COULD BE A STORY ABOUT SWIMMING

Such a hot day; one of those rare, perfect days of summer. Your parents drowsy with sandwiches, stretched out in the collapsible chairs Dad wrestled out of the car. Your little brother curling in your mother's lap, and although she says he's far too old to be such a baby, her arms grip him tight. And you, stepping into the river, chill sharpening your breath to a point.

"Don't be long, sweetie," your mother is calling, eyes half-closed against the glare.

"Don't go far!" cries your father. You wave, inviting him in. "In a moment," he says, voice muffled, eyelids flopping. You've never understood how he can fall asleep so fast.

The water is delicious, your limbs sliding without effort. Fish shimmering, mosquitoes whining, trees leaning over the shadows under their branches, and you are swimming now, easy and strong, breath glittering in your lungs. How you've grown! You have never felt so alive, ripple-thighed and powering the weight of yourself forwards, and although you know he won't be there, you pause to see if your father is following.

The lowering sun is blurring your vision. You tread water, shade your eyes and squint, but there's no sign of your family. Everything has gone: your parents, the chairs, the picnic. There's a tall man on the bank, with a scraggly beard and tie-dyed T-shirt. You know it's your brother, even though it's impossible because he was a toddler when you waved goodbye only a few moments ago. He's jumping up and down, one arm sweeping in an urgent semaphore, free hand cupped round his mouth. Whatever he's shouting, the words are drowned in the river's gathering thunder.

You don't know what possessed you to leave, and fight to turn around, but the current punches you in the chest and it's only now you're trying to go back you realise your muscles aren't what they were. The chill that was refreshing is sticking knives into your lungs. The river has taken over, shoving you onwards.

Spiralling further and further downstream, away and further away, you tell yourself you're the strongest swimmer in your class; try to believe it although the drone of insects is loud enough to drown out thought.

Your bones creak, joints sear and shriek. The breast stroke that came with ease is now agony. You didn't know pain could be like this, consuming body and mind and blanking out all other considerations. You are fighting and losing, fighting and losing, feet slipping and tearing on the rocks, grappling for each rattling wheezing breath.

You don't want to look at your body, because of what you might see. You look anyway: shrivelled arms and legs, swollen knees and ankles, hipbones that jut at strange angles. An old woman is wearing your body; a stranger who has crept in, stolen everything and left you with a bag of sticks. You wonder how this could happen, when was the moment things started to change and why you can't get back to where you started.

Everything is racing past so quickly. There's hardly time to blink. You whirl in helpless circles, flailing and grasping for tree-roots, anything to slow you down. Ahead, the river is boiling as it vanishes over the falls.

LIFE ON EARTH

She first notices the odour when locking up, her nightly ritual since he died fifteen years ago. She gives the key a firm twist, grinding the bones in her wrist. Aches and pains. Bugger them all. They're not foremost in her mind. That would be the smell. It reminds her of stables: animal sweat and breathed-out hay.

She doesn't fancy a cup of tea, not with the metallic taste under her tongue again. She unplugs the kettle and struggles up the stairs. It's probably the effort, but she'd swear it's hotter on the landing. The grassy aroma is stronger, too.

She stumbles to the bedroom and plonks herself down, taking deep gulps of sweltering air. She stretches to turn on the bedside lamp, but can't reach the switch. It'll keep. It's not like she's going to get lost in her own room, however dark.

It's only then she realises she's still wearing her Wellington boots. Why she didn't take them off in the kitchen is anyone's guess. Perhaps it explains the smell: she pictures herself treading cat mess into the living room carpet, on each and every stair and now her rug.

Damn and blast.

Except it isn't cat mess; she knows *that* stink of old. This is a herbivore scent, and just like that, she thinks of the David Attenborough programme about African grasslands, as clear as if she watched it just before she came upstairs: lions chasing gazelles; giraffes graceful as dhows.

The more she sniffs, the more she's inclined to think it's rather pleasant. She shakes herself. Nice or not, she ought to take the boots downstairs and lay them on newspaper ready for cleaning in the morning. Problems are easier to solve in daylight, and there's precious little of that at this dismal time of year. Winter is a bleak season when everyone and everything paddles out on a tide that doesn't come back in again. December was when her George went. *What is it about Christmas and people dying?* She wonders.

She sighs, lifts her left foot and grips the boot, when something stirs behind her.

She ought to be afraid. After all, it's what we all fear: to get into bed and find something there that shouldn't be. Her breathing remains steady, her heartbeat also. She sees no reason why she shouldn't carry on with what she was doing, so gives the boot a shove. It slides off more easily than expected and falls to the floor with a soft, un-boot-like plop.

Whatever is on the bed shifts again, timidly, as if it doesn't want to disturb her.

"You're not any bother," she says, and feels a certain tension in the room relax.

The air smoothes out gratefully, a weight descends to her shoulder, and a warm cheek presses against hers. Long eyelashes flutter up and down. Loud but tender breath, and that powerful aroma of the veldt. She turns her head a fraction. By the faint light trickling through the curtains from the street, she can just make out an elegant snout.

The giraffe exhales a lengthy savannah breath.

She raises a hand and lays it shyly upon the bony ridge above the soft nostrils. The creature snuffles and wraps a muscular foreleg around her, squeezing gently. She never imagined an animal as gangly could be so comfortingly affectionate. It's not logical, of course, but she thinks of her mother, who bore no resemblance to a giraffe whatsoever.

The giraffe lets out a series of tiny snorts, no louder than rain on a window, and she realises it is laughing. *What a lovely notion*, she thinks, as the room descends into complete darkness and she floats out on her own tide. *A giraffe, laughing.*

QUINQUIREME OF NINEVEH

Dad and I are doing the dishes: him washing, me drying. It's the routine we slip into after Sunday lunch, however much he insists that, as his guest, I should sit down. He doesn't like me to lift a finger, even if it's only to wrap a tea towel around the cutlery. Today, I win the battle.

There have been plenty where I wasn't victorious. I inherited the stubborn way Dad folds his arms and sticks out his chin; his determination to wrestle bad luck into better and keep going. It's no surprise that sparks flew while I was growing up, all of our rough edges grinding against each other. We both learned that time can heal all fires, if both parties are prepared to fight the flames before they rage out of control. No regrets.

He scrubs gravy from a plate, I swab it dry. We joke about the poems he learned by heart at school: Young Lochinvar coming out of the West, boys on burning decks, quinquiremes of Nineveh. While I'm laughing, he tells me his news.

He leans against the sink unit, his only concession to being eighty, whereas I have to grab a chair and sit down. I'm dizzy with the impact of new words to learn: *prognosis, aggressive, metastasis*. I can't look him in the eye. Not yet.

"I can't beat this one," he says. "Not for want of trying."

I haul myself upright, grab a fistful of spoons from the drainer, dry them slowly. So much to say, no idea where to begin. Dad does the talking for us both.

"Anyway. Poetry. I'm a Dirty British Coaster," he says, grinning. He elbows me gently and I manage to return the smile.

I inherited the silver lining of his smile, too. "With a salt-caked smoke stack. Though I gave up ciggies years ago."

Not soon enough.

The unspoken words hover between us. We gaze out of the kitchen window at the field beyond the damp garden. It is largely mud. A cloud of spray, too fine to fall as rain, obscures the boundary line of poplars. Two horses slump under blankets, heads drooping.

"Poor blighters are left outside in all weathers," he mutters. A muscle in his cheek ticks as he scrubs at a blob of fat. "Blasted woman doesn't feed them. Thinks grass is enough, even in winter."

The horses look miserable, velvet muzzles lowered to the ground. As I watch, I realise it's not melancholy. They're bowing in honour of the ghostly fifty-oared Carthaginian galley nosing through the line of trees and into the paddock. In fact, they only move aside when the huge barge is on the verge of mowing them down. It breasts out of the mist, sails across the field and comes to a graceful stop a few feet shy of the garden hedge. Dad lets go of the dishcloth and it lands in the bowl with a plop.

"Oh," he says breathlessly, placing his hand over his heart. "Will you look at that, now."

I can't look anywhere else. I lay down the spoons with care, glad I wasn't drying a plate.

"That's... big," I reply. The curved bow stretches the height of the house, blocking the thin December light. I crane my neck to work out how long it is, but the stern is lost in foggy drizzle. It is made of a deliciously dark wood. "Is that Cedar of Lebanon?" I gabble. "Is that what a quinquireme looks like?"

Dad jerks his head in something that could be a *yes*. "I'm off to find out," he says.

He dries his hands and shuffles to the back door. I follow, curious to discover what he'll say to the crew of a 2,000-year-old longship invading the peace of his afternoon. I wonder if he'll shout. I can't remember the last time I heard my father raise his voice in anger; not since I was a teenager and we threw away twenty years outdoing each other in pig-headedness. I was so stupid I thought myself the winner because I left home on the dot of eighteen and never returned. Neither of us won. No one wins the game of squandered decades. When I said I had no regrets I was lying.

"I'm sorry," I say to his retreating back. "I wasted so much time."

He's moving faster than I thought possible, what with his knackered chest. He springs over the hedge and across the meadow. I struggle to keep up; breath heavy in my lungs, ears whistling.

A bearded man peers over the side of the ship, teeth glinting in a curved moon of a smile. He says something incomprehensible.

"I don't speak ancient Babylonian," I say to Dad. "Neither do you."

Against all expectations, my father is nodding as though he understands every word. The man reaches down over the gunwale and Dad stretches up to meet the handclasp. The sides of the vessel tower so high there's no way their fingers can touch, but touch they do. The captain hoists Dad upward and he leaps onboard, sixty of his eighty years falling from him like an unwanted coat.

Dad!" I cry. "Don't go! You're my Dirty British Coaster!"

He doesn't turn; doesn't wave. "It's bigger than I imagined," I hear him say, as he strolls along the deck. "It goes on forever."

The oars stir the thickening rain, and the boat reverses slowly until it is lost in the fog of where it came from. I clear up the dishes, remembering everything I should have said while I had the chance. I always think of the right thing to say when people are too far away to hear.

In the sodden meadow, the horses are waiting for the weather to change. Wise creatures, they know nothing lasts forever, not even the rain.

HOWEVER FAR SHE RUNS AWAY
FROM HOME

My mother lives in a house full of gravestones. Every morning, she vacuums around their beds and washes their faces clean of any lichen that bloomed overnight, until they look fresh as the day of their funerals.

I'm sure there are more each time I visit, sculpted from gleaming black marble or sober slate. As a peace offering, I'm wearing the powder-blue sweater she knitted, even though it chafes around my throat.

"Aren't they taking up a lot of space?" I say, in my softest cotton-wool voice.

"They're no trouble," she replies, as I turn sideways to squeeze my way to the settee. "And they're good listeners."

I pretend not to hear the accusation. I'm tingling for a cigarette, poke one between my lips. She glances over her shoulder to where they loom, and hisses, "Show some respect."

"They are stone, Mother," I say, taking the first deep inhalation. The slab at my elbow glitters steel. "Heaps of rock."

"Shh," she says. "They're good companions. *They* don't cause me a moment's worry."

She strokes the closest like a cat and it butts its head into her hand. I didn't know stone could purr. I shake my head. I'm imagining things.

"It wouldn't hurt you to have a few."

I tingle with the urge to growl, *Why?*

I spent years extracting myself from her crush and smother. I've no intention of weighing myself down again. I give a non-committal smile. Although I say I'm not hungry, she bustles into the kitchen, negotiating her way through the maze. She returns with a pot of tea and a plate of sandwiches, crusts sliced off and cut into triangles the size to suit a doll's picnic. I sip the tea: weak, milky, three sugars. The opposite of what I drink and she knows it.

"Now, that's a proper cup of tea for a lady," she says, without looking at me.

I set down the cup. "I can't... it's too sweet."

I try one of the sandwiches. The bread is filled with a dense gluey filling, like chewing papier-mâché. I spit a lump onto my palm. Clotted shreds of pastel tissue.

"Is this confetti?" I ask, picking bits out of my teeth.

"You need to eat," she says. "I don't know what you girls call food but it's not enough." She blows her nose into a lace-edged handkerchief. "Would it kill you to make me happy, just once?" she sniffs. "Can't you bring yourself to do the tiniest thing for your mother, who never asks for anything?"

I tread warily. If I say what I really think about her continual hints to get settled with a nice man, I'll get the full production. She'll start sobbing how all she wants is my happiness, how a daughter's cruelty can reduce your heart to rubble, and how I can't possibly understand because I haven't got children of my own.

I make another valiant attempt to tackle the sickly brew, hoping to wash down the words I've been bottling up for years. The saccharine stew bubbles and seethes, as heavy on my stomach as the claggy sandwich.

"*They* listen to me," she wails, patting the grave slabs. "*They* don't go running off and leaving me on my own. *They* don't make me cry myself to sleep at night." She drifts around the room. "Why won't you give me the grandchildren I deserve? You're not too old. Not yet."

Before I can think of a reply, she frisks out her phone and snaps a photo of me staring into my lap, shoulders hunched, defeated again. She starts to gather up the tea-things.

"Well then, darling. I'll see you on Sunday," she says brightly. "I do look forward to our little chats." She cups her hand around my cheek, her palm calloused from polishing headstones till she can see her face in them. "You're such a good girl. I wish every mother could have a daughter like you."

My head spins. I'm hemmed in by gravestones pert and attentive as bridesmaids. Each time I visit, they shuffle a little closer. Each time, it's harder to get away.

UNDER THE WATER, THE DEAD ARE STILL MOVING

You're barely the height of your mother's hip when she takes you to witness the water sacrifice. The clan gathers at the border of land and lake, plumes of damp air flowing from their mouths. The breast of land-not-land squeezes copper milk over your toes. It takes four men to carry the bronze cauldron to the end of the jetty, oaken planks bending beneath them. It takes two more to tilt the vessel on its side. Sweat runs down their chins as they tip the muddled ale and honey into the pool, where it spreads in a pale cloak.

I am hauled along on my knees, arms roped behind my back. They slather me with crimson ochre, stuff my mouth with a mulch of seeds, twist the garrotte and cut my throat to be completely sure. Chanting rises to a shriek as they try to mask the hiss of angry water as they toss me in. I must be destroyed, for my eyes have seen the secret way. Not the whale-road to the sunset, nor any land of earth and ice. I know of a more tantalising realm.

Beware, my child. They watch for one like you.
It is too late for me, but not for you.

Mother grips your little paw, the squeeze-release spelling silence, watchfulness. You see the man dragged to the shivery brink, his skin red and gleaming as an evening sun. You peer closer. It's not only the scarlet of ochre. His body is radiant on the inside, like yours. He swings his head from side to side. At first, you think of a cornered beast, but no. He is searching. His gaze locks with yours and he smiles, for you are the object of his seeking. His voice sings in your head, gentler than your mother's sweetest lullaby, more terrifying than your father's wildest storm.

They call me holy, call me sacrifice, call it honouring the gods. They sigh, and say I am too holy for this world. Say they are easing my path into the sacred realm, which is more fitting to my nature. They wipe dry eyes, bleat a ragbag of excuses while I burn, unfettered and ungovernable. I refuse to kneel to them: priests who dabble in the entrails of crows; shadow men who envy anyone they cannot twist to their own ends. Here is the truth: I am too dangerous to live. I outshine their snivelling glow. I dance between worlds while they remain mudbound. I shine with the light of strangeness. I shine free.

Beware, my child. They watch for one like you.
It is too late for me, but not for you.

Priestesses pour libations from the horns of cattle; priests bellow hymns. Warriors form a circle around the man. They thump their spears and grunt like wild pigs, but cannot muffle his cries. Flash of a blade. The silence that follows is worse than the screaming. Mother hangs onto you so fiercely your knuckles grind together. You do not let out a sound; arrange your features into blandness. You are already learning the importance of concealment.

I sink into the sloshing belly of the god. Where better to exile the ones who burn with the wildfire of waywardness? My flesh melts into sludge, sour as the bitter herbs our people chew in famine years. The graveyard dogs cower, tails hugged between their legs, whining for mercy. Even for their scavenging appetites, I am too rank.

Beware, my child. They watch for ones like you.
It is too late for me, but not for you.

You dance to your daddy, sparkle for your mammy. Stick your thumb into the porridge-pot and make it bubble. With a kiss, you spark heat into soaking wood. Until the day shadows flood your home. Neighbours pointing, whispering. Your parents questioned, threatened. From then on, your mother forbids the flickering games, hums lullabies warning concealment. "But Mama," you say, "don't you love me anymore?" She hugs you till you squeal. "Beware, my child," she says. "They watch for ones like you."

In life, breath held me together. In this sodden grave, I am breathless. Flesh and shadow torn apart, my name swallowed into earth and forgotten. Even shrivelled into a sack of bones, I can scent the heat of one who burns as I do.

Beware, my child. They watch for ones like you.
It is too late for me, but not for you.

Your mother tells you to tamp down the smallest ember. Slathers you with river clay to blur any trace of inner light that might betray your secret. You play a game of hide-and-never-seek, hold yourself in so tight your glimmer is invisible, even to the birds. You don't understand why your power is deemed dangerous. You could warm a room, your clan, your shivering, shuddering land.

For the sake of this girl, I rise from my water-grave. Knit bones and meat into something like a man, and drizzle my way to her little cot. My limbs drip and stream. Ice rolls off my back and thighs in fat clouds. I weep tears of brine, stretch out my hand and whisper into her sleeping. She is wonderful and brave, and does not let out one cry.

Beware, my child. They watch for ones like you.
It is too late for me, but not for you.

While the family sleeps, you unfurl wings of flame and fly to the heart of the forest. Rising from his muddy bed, a shining ghost takes your hand, and together you dance out the long and lovely hours till morning. You are shooting stars, a river of lights to wrap around the heavens. You know better than to tell your mother. Each night, you lie upon your bed of straw, open the door to your dreams and greet your radiant companion.

They call us unholy, unwholesome. Fear and jealousy will always invent an excuse to wipe us from existence. Do not let them turn their eyes upon you next. Pay heed. There is much to learn, and quickly. I shall go with you and be your guide. I shall teach you to study cuckoos, the way they pretend they are ordinary birds, until old enough to flee the nest. I shall teach you to study foxes, the way they tread as silent as the darkness. The way they outrun danger.

Beware, my child. They watch for one like you.
Watch and be ready, I shall return to you.

You listen to your lessons. Learn how to bury fire, how to carry it night after night, sheltered in your heart. Learn how to bide your time, counting the seasons till you are grown enough to leave. Then, you rise early and walk from your cold and heartless land. You keep walking till the day you look over your shoulder and realise your homestead is so far behind as to be lost. You meet new friends, for you are not alone. You never were. With each league you gather fierce and fiery wanderers. You are a rowdy family of sisters, brothers, neithers, others, each one of you roaring raucous songs. So much has been lost, but not everything. It is not too late.

We are unruly as the greyscape of the outer ocean, furious as the scorching blaze that bursts from earth. We are torches to light the underworld. We shall walk together, off the edge of the fearful world and into new.

Rejoice, my child. There are legions like you.

The way ahead is difficult. You aren't there yet. The weather is stormy and sometimes knocks you sideways. You'd not trade one gristly mouthful of your brave new world for all the tempting honey of the old. You find strength you never dared believe in, your gaze fixed to the horizon and the hope that shines there. You are fierce and ferocious, beyond anyone's command. You fill the skies with angry laughter. This time is yours. Not once upon a time, but always.

You weave worlds from words, build them strong and stronger with each new history. Stronger than hate, than fear. Your new-found-land is on no map. It is a homeland you carry, making and re-making with each step along the way. And, as he promised, at your side strides your drowned companion, keeping watch over the living.

I shall never desert you. I speak in the lightning's fork, in the thunder's roar. Tell my tale and I will live forever. I lie smiling, folded in earth and water. My words howl in the wind, my heart a quenchless fire.

Rejoice, my child. There are legions like you.

CAUGHT IN THE CROSSHAIRS

The stakeout is dragging. Minutes feel like hours. Across the street, cops lick the frosting off doughnuts, crumple coffee cups in their fists, cameras trained on your apartment.

The mailman delivers letters and packages; carefully resealed, but you can tell. You pace the room, curtains thrown open. You have nothing to hide.

You can't understand what's taking them so long. Each night, you stand at the window, unbutton your shirt, heart an easy target.

For God's sake. You can't make it any clearer. Where to aim. What they have to do.

CLIMBING WALL

She prides herself on being a supportive friend: a shoulder to lean on, a listening ear at the end of the phone. A tall woman, only forbidding at first glance; she likes the feeling of people scaling her defences so much that she makes it easy, attaching colourful grips of moulded plastic for them to clutch. They are so grateful. Call her their best friend ever.

In return, their weight holds her steady. Mother always stressed the importance of service to others. Besides, it's only a matter of time before they take their own initiative. As soon as they climb to the top of her wall and see the amazing view, they'll rush back down to construct their own.

It's not hard. She did it.

She doesn't understand why they seem content to cling. Not that she minds, but surely, they'd prefer to be independent? She must be doing something wrong. She puts up notices printed in block capitals, *THIS WAY DOWN*. Waits for the highest to abseil back to the ground.

But next morning, the crowd of climbers is just as dense. They grin through the windows of her eyes, waving *hello*. She tries to get her fingernails underneath one and prise him loose, but he's fastened tight as a limpet. Surely, she's running out of room; but still they swarm, two or three deep in places, clambering on each other's shoulders and hanging on.

She's exhausted from carrying the extra load. Leans dangerously. When was the last time she slept through the night without waking at 4am, forced to eavesdrop their muttering whimpers? And that other sound: a hundred thumbs being sucked at once.

"Please," she says. "Maybe one or two of you could go?"

"You said you'd always be there for us," they moan. "You promised."

She can barely breathe. She unscrews the bright plastic handhold closest to her mouth and takes in a lungful of air, the first for weeks without sucking in someone's fingers, or a ponytail. There's a thud. She doesn't know if it's the handhold dropping to the floor, or one of the hangers-on. She doesn't want to look.

"Oh!" they cry. "How can you do this? We thought you were our friend."

She's a fool. She should never have made it so easy; should unbolt the handholds closest to the ground, dissuade them from starting to climb. Too late now. She's buckling but can't bear the idea of prising their fingers loose, the thought of their limp bodies piling around her ankles.

Whining in her ears. High-pitched, unending.

She sleeps fitfully. Dreams of empty walls.

THE PLEDGE

On Friday, he hands the ticket to the pawnbroker and you are returned to his keeping. He touches his lips to your cheek.

"The children are excited. They are full of anticipation for the return of their Mama," he murmurs. "As am I."

His moustache smells of ammonia. The marshy dampness of his hands.

You remember the perfection of his dress, his collars as pristine at the close of the day as at the moment he draws them from the press. You walk at his side, concentrating on where to place your feet. The afternoon sun is bright, forcing the shadows into a retreat, lumping underneath the pollarded elms.

"Mama!" cry the children, patting you with small, clean hands.

"Careful," he chides them. "She must not get creased or dirty."

"We remember, Papa," they say eagerly, licking puffy lips.

Atop the pianoforte, the photograph of your wedding day winks at you from its polished silver frame. Your hair combed into a halo. *You are an angel,* he said at the breakfast gathering. *Do angels have red hair?* you replied. You were so innocent, then.

"Mama," say the children, with urgent voices. "Make us a cake. Now. Red velvet, filled with apricot cream."

You obey. You have not forgotten that children must eat savoury as well as sweet, and so you prepare a chicken pie. Your fingertips glisten with butter and chopped tarragon.

Next morning, you fry bacon and pancakes. You make lunch. You make love. You do the laundry. The lisping voices of the children, saying *Mama, Mama,* over and over. You cook a three-course dinner for five of his work colleagues and their wives. The following evening, a three-course dinner for five different men. Their wives look the same: the blank expressions, the glazed stare.

While you serve coffee and the almond wafers that are your specialty, he talks of his plans for another son, a holiday in the mountains, the window blinds that are so fashionable this season. After the guests have made their goodbyes, with compliments upon your cooking, you scrape leftover cream sauce into the sink and think of your quiet shelf in the pawnbroker's cabinet.

Only a few more hours before you are returned.

Next Friday, you promise yourself, you will not come when he calls your name.

THE THIRD-FAVOURITE WIFE
OF THE EMPEROR

At the hoist of the red lantern, she draws the curtain of her cuff across her face, so she does not pollute The Emperor with her unworthy gaze. At His approach, she invokes the spirit of the nightingale and trills gratitude for His gifts: a toothpick, a sprinkle of caraway, a pot of foxgloves. Basking in His Divine Radiance, she conjures herself from bird into the squeezed crawl of silkworm grub; grinds her brow in dust made holy by His heels.

Small wife. Humble. The neat brown *cheep* of her agreements, her praise-songs for His Majesty, the Great Sage, Equal of Heaven. She has memorised the hundred righteous positions of a woman: the peony, the dog, the spatchcocked pigeon. She plants incense sticks before Kuan Yin, sheaves of them, pleading for mercy that she may bear ripe sons and be spared the yoke of intelligence.

Most all of all, she studies the goddess's most important lesson: how to keep her skull attached to her neck. Every month there is a new wife. She is but one of many choices. In the cage of her head, she tends dreams of butterflies. The bars are so narrow that no finger, however celestial, can poke through and flatten the tiny creatures.

I AM IRT-IRW, DAUGHTER OF PEDAMENOPE!

The mummy of Irt-irw has been on display at The Great North museum in Newcastle on Tyne since 1884

I remember a soft mouth smelling of new dates. He kissed my hand five times; once for each finger and the thumb, called me his plot of ground planted with flowers, a paradise in which to wander. We ran amongst the incense trees in my father's garden, their thirsty feet sunk into muddy pits.

"You are my vineyard," he said. "Let me drink from you."

The sand warm beneath my feet. His hand on my belly. The daughter I bore. This, I remember.

One morning it grew dark and did not lighten. I heard him say, "She fell. I could not wake her."

The sky lifted the corner of her skirt and I plunged my face into its dark folds, cried for my mama. The Goddess buried me in the night of her monstrous thighs. My thumb crept towards my mouth, and I found it warm and comforting.

The Goddess hushed my weeping for the seventy days I lay with the embalmers. Their hands were busy in every part of me: I would have blushed if had I not been dead. They cut me open, scooped out my entrails, my liver and my lungs, packed them into jars stoppered with the heads of beasts. They whisked my brain to cream. I would not be needing it. My heart they left me. I coffer it between my ribs. Now I can only recall things I loved and things I hated. I cannot measure time, nor the length of my arm. So, forgive me if my memory is selective.

Then they laid me in a crib of salt till I was parched, swaddled me in linen, cradled me in this pretty box. My tears dried up. My family carried me to my tomb, waving flowers beneath my chin, although the scent had been taken into a distant room. In any case, I was drowsy enough. I did not need lotus blooms. I heard hair torn out, like barley ripped from the fields by robbers. The weeping of my children sounded like laughter, and I grew cold.

The priest struck my wooden lips, but the mourners' wailing was so loud no-one heard me shout, *I do not want to leave you!* They bricked me in, smoothed plaster on the door. Left bread. A bowl of meat. Cheap beer in good jars. I gulped it all. Tasted grit between my teeth.

For a short while, they brought food. I grew hungry. Around me, fat ducks quacked in the reed thicket daubed on the walls. I could hear the painted offering table creak with its weight of loaves fresh from the oven. Another table groaned beneath its load of roasted lamb; another heaped with jars of beer, and cakes, and figs, and dates, and fried garlic and grilled chicken.

Ghost water fluttered in my mouth. I was surrounded by food I could not reach. I scrabbled at the inside of my box until my Soul showed me how to break free and leap up through the lid. I staggered through watercolour marshes, grabbed a squawking bird, crammed it whole into my mouth without stopping to pluck it. I licked the pictures off the walls, swallowed every mouthful quick as a jackal. There was no time to chew.

Still, I couldn't sleep.

In my continual night, I heard my husband whisper, *you are my vineyard. Let me drink from you.* A strange voice answered: his new wife, fingers sticky with dough. My fury beat against the door of my tomb, found its way through and swept across the river to the house that was once mine. I filled the mouth of the wind and blew sand into their flour so that their teeth ground down and became a constant agony. I sharpened the teeth of the desert and bit their new son's heel with scorpions. Feasted on their sorrow. I became hard as ebony.

Then there was the day light fell through the bricked-up door. I thought, *He is sorry: he has sent her away. He cannot live without me. Has come to lie down at my side.* But they were robbers, nervous hands fumbling for my bracelets, the carved beetle I carried over my heart. I saw how thin they were. Hungrier than me. But I'd bribed important demons to stand at my head and feet.

"This is Irt-irw, daughter of Pedamenope!"

Their shrieking sent the thieves away with my jewellery.

Sand choked my tomb. I lay quiet, counted my fingers, made do with silence. The river was always there, coiling round the edge of the village, bright as a knife blade. The passing of a hundred generations dimmed my taste for anger. I forgot my husband's name, as did everyone on earth. It's hard to stay furious with a man whose name you do not recall. Now there's not a splinter left of his lying body. And I'm the one telling this story.

Light flared again. Perhaps the Gods had come to fetch me? But these men were worse than my two-thousand-year-old hunger, worse than the embalmers, worse than the thieves who at least said prayers to banish the demons.

"I am Irt-irw, daughter of Pedamenope!"

These robbers did not hear me, did not believe in curses, did not tremble. There was not much left to steal, so they took my body, the box I lay in. Scraped the ointment from my feet, tore the flowers from my breast. Chipped the paintings from the walls. Could they not see I'd sucked out all the marrow?

They hauled me from my tomb. Packed me like a crate of pickled fish and shipped me north, across the Great Green and further, to a country where water turns to stone in winter. I had no Gods to protect me, because they could not sail this far. These men unravelled me from my wrappings. Hung me from a hook like a hide waiting for the tanner. They think I am too old for modesty, but they are mistaken. See how I clutch myself where life begins.

I rediscovered anger, and how sweet it tastes.

I am not asleep: let no-one persuade you otherwise. I see you poor ghosts nibble at the edges of my dreams, your distant voices the sound of bees caught in a pot, and of as little consequence. You are watching me now, comparing my breasts to leather satchels, how my eyes are shrivelled up like last year's grapes. I will not even lift my eyelids to glare at you. You are so pale; wrapped up against a cold I never knew.

I am too busy smiling to talk to you. You cannot take my name. *I am Irt-irw, daughter of Pedamenope.* Say a woman's name and she shall live forever. I shall live forever. Not you. I've watched one hundred of your thieving generations turn to slime.

CIRCUS OF LOVE

Roll up, roll up! The greatest show on earth and you're the star attraction. Tonight's the night to show him what he's missing: the man of your dreams, your prince come true.

Act One: a rootin' tootin' rodeo. He's the Lone Ranger and you're his little chickadee.

He gallops past: aims, fires, and shoots the cigarette from between your teeth. Hi ho Silver and away, tipping you head-over-heels into the dirt. But he was meant to sweep you onto his saddle. You check the script. There, on page two. It doesn't matter. The show must go on.

So what if you can't lasso his eye with cowgirl charm? Snap of the fingers and you're Queen of the Air, the human cannonball. Crash bang wallop, what a diva! Crowned with stars, you streak a comet's tail, sequin constellations glittering your thighs. You'll show him how high true love can fly. He is your sun, the gravity that pulls you close. You open your arms wide as sesame, stretch to take his hand, but his grasp is butter. You slip and fall.

Quick as a flash, you turn the plummet into an angel's dive. Oh! The applause as you toss aside the safety net. Soft landings are for losers. What's a broken bone between lovers? He's such a tease. You're meant for each other. He doesn't know it yet, that's all. Next time for sure.

On with the motley! Your beloved turns his spotlight beam on you, drives you towards the Hoop of Flame, cracking his whip. Only those who've never tasted love would call it cruelty when he snaps the lash around your heart. Besides, the cuts are too small to see. Any minute now he'll call you his glamorous assistant. You dance into the fire. If your eyes sting, it's with tears of joy. The crowd's cheering is loud enough to drown the reek of burning hair. Not your fault. And never his.

You can't stop. Not now you're so close. Quick shift of costume, one that takes years off you. You are Death-defying Delilah Dentata, plunging your head into the lion's mouth. This'll bring the audience to its feet. You stare down the barrel of its throat. Pick meat from other women's hearts out of its teeth.

You swore you'd never lose your head. Where is he, your ringmaster, the only man you love? Where is the music of his cat-o'-nine-tails? He doesn't mean to hurt you. Every time he says sorry. Promises he'll never do it again.

With every turn round Love's circus ring, you shed light, hope, life. You don't understand. You're giving him your all: you've swallowed swords, danced tightropes, twisted yourself in knots to fit the shape of his desire. Why won't he drop to one knee, pop that question?

The crowd are shifting in their seats, eyeing the exit signs, and yawning. The first tomato explodes at your feet.

"Wait!" you cry.

Time for the Grand Finale. You step into the ring and spread your arms. There's roaring in your ears. You've given almost everything for love. He ain't seen nothin' yet. You climb into the six-foot box and close the lid. Ladies and gentleman. Prepare yourselves. The Lady Sawn in Half.

PIRATE MOLLY

We've not been the same since Molly arrived on the ward. She roused us from our doldrums, roared a gale between our ears. She reminded us how to draw our outlines firm and thick; fill ourselves to the brim with the brightest crayons in the box. We fly our flags wild with colours we forgot were ours.

Eye-patched with cataracts, and hammocked in an incontinence pad, Molly peglegs the corridors, faster than any of the midshipman nurses who feed us, wipe us, turn us, fill us full to rattling with sleeping pills.

Four in the morning, and all to plan, Molly shakes us from sleep.

"Time is short, and only a fool spends it snoring," she hisses, her Sunday hat screwed sideways on her head and a plastic knife between her teeth.

I don't need telling twice. I'm ready, gussied up in my best, or what's left of it after the long years marooned in this prison hulk. For too long, I've been lost at sea, stranded on one of the chairs that line the Day Room. Surrounded by visitors with escape in their eyes, who yawn at the yarns I spin. Well-meaning folk who wrinkle their noses at my seaweed smell, whose eyes look straight through me and out the other side.

"X marks the spot," says Molly.

We totter under the bilge-green glow of the Fire Exit sign, eager for adventure.

"Hoist the mizzen mast," she cackles, passing the word down the line of us bare-arsed beauties. Our shrivelled moons wax and wane, wax and wane again.

"Dance!" cries Molly. She kidnaps my hand and I hang on as she leads me into a waltz. She is a witch, who spirits my legs back to life. "Sing!" cries Molly.

My voice creaks its rusty gears and the words come, loud and luscious. "Pieces of eight. Yo ho ho and a bottle of rum!"

The night staff line up, arms linked in a press gang. Wondering where we got the fire to misbehave, we skeletons with soup on our breasts and minds that ought to behave as soft as cream cheese.

"Away with you," they say. "Come on now, back to bed. Tsk tsk, what are we doing here?"

When we don't buckle under, they get rougher, telling us we are *naughty girls*.

We are pirates with no future, no land to call our home. Everything that we once were is buried on an island we sailed from a long time hence. The map is blotched and burned around the edges. All we have are our skull and crossbones bodies, our tattered sails of nightgowns, our bruise tattoos. We have our keel-hauled memories bulging with barnacles. And we have Molly.

I am a mutiny, small but fierce. I've seen enough of war to know the battles are never done. My victories grow thinner, along with my bones, but they shine bright. Dead men tell no tales, but I have a stretch ahead of me before I am fitted into Davy Jones's Locker. We are all walking the plank between this world and the next. Molly shows me how to kick up my heels and dance the rest of that short way.

THE ACT OF CLINGING CRACKS AND BLEEDS
IF NOT ATTENDED TO,
LIKE KNUCKLES IN WINTER

Whatever the weather, she digs the garden, moving plants around. Mother said a plant won't thrive until rooted in the right spot. Wherever she positions the hole, however often she feeds blood, fish and bone, they grow half-hearted.

All summer she tends and nurtures: patient for growth, for them to settle into home. She sweet-talks and they ignore her. Her capacity for love should be enough, she screams. Threatens with magazine articles about artificial grass, backyards buried under concrete and plastic decking. The garden shrivels. On her knees in the dirt, she begs for forgiveness.

GOOD WITH WORDS, BAD WITH NUMBERS

It's what you told me on our second date. You said it was cute; said it was proof we made the perfect couple.

"I'm good with words," you purred. "You are bad with numbers."

It was your first lie.

My eyes were so bedazzled with stars and shadows that I believed you rather than believing the truth of myself. I doubted all the evidence, where I aced every maths exam, got A Star Plus.

Which is why, four years, three months and sixteen days later, I'm throwing things into a suitcase. Things, things, things. All that's left are things.

I'm telling myself this is it. This time I won't come back.

Eight shirts.

"Should you be doing that?" you ask me, arms behind your head and showing no signs of getting out of bed.

You're waiting for me to crumple, unpack the bag and get back into bed. You've watched this circle dance a number of times I'm too ashamed to calculate. Over and over, I loop around to where I started. Desperation does that to a person. 24% of times, I made it as far as the street. Raised my arms to the sky, praying for angels to grab hold and rescue me. I wanted to pretend you weren't waiting, swirling a glass of Chardonnay. Wanted a little longer in the city's half-dark, to relish the shadows' curl and crawl. All I heard was the bad-tempered growl of cats, edging each other out of the back alley.

I remember all the times I've returned, to find you with your feet up and humming *I Will Survive* under your breath. Knowing that if I complained, you would laugh and say, *Who says I was singing about you?* before breaking into *You're So Vain*. The way you said I'd never leave, because I couldn't manage one solitary single day on my own.

Five pairs of socks, balled in matching pairs.

As a kid, maths saved me. Fractions never let me down. Whatever didn't add up at home, I could trust algebra to come out right in the end. Maths had rules that held steady when I leaned on them. The sum of the square on the hypotenuse was always equal to the sum of the squares of the two shorter sides; the eight-times table did not say one thing and mean another.

Words were another matter. Like the bicycle I got the Christmas I was nine. I pedalled it sunrise to sunset, my heart bursting with pride. Boxing Day dawned, Dad took the bike back to the shop and I learned that joy lasts less than 24 hours; learned the unreliability of the word *present*.

My favourite jacket, the velvet one you said you'd get for my birthday and I bought with my own money.

I watch you pick a bit of last night's dinner from between your teeth. Out on the street, cars are revving out of driveways, leaving car-sized spaces and racing to car-sized spaces elsewhere. You're talking about how you're the only person you know who learnt Latin, and what a pointless exercise that was. How, no matter how hard you try, you've never forgotten how to decline verbs. *Amo, amas, amat, amamus, amatis, amant*, like those love songs where all you remember is the chorus.

Another of your stories. Like the time you said, *Forever*. Your forever lasted two months, seven days and fourteen hours. When you got on your knees and swore I was the only one, you meant I was the only one of many; the only one in the room at that moment; the only one falling for the lies. You are a magician of words, pulling them from your sleeve and flourishing them like bunches of fake flowers, convinced I'll be distracted by the pretty petals. Not this time.

My favourite pair of trainers, pressed sole to sole.

Ten tee shirts, rolled tight.

I had it backwards all along. I've always been great with numbers. My problem was believing your claim that two-plus-two-equals-five. Like every winner who thinks they're way out in front, you've grown lazy. Your lies are tarnished around the edges where once they sparkled, so bright I could see my face in them, smiling with dreams come true. You warped my dreams to suit your purpose. Maths can save me again. No. I can save myself.

I zip the case closed.

"See ya," you say, in your smug and lazy drawl.

You fold back the duvet and swing upright, pad to the kitchen to make coffee. 47% of times the grind of roasted beans tugs me back.

Ten small steps out of the bedroom. Twelve steps to the front door. Easy numbers I can understand. I close the door behind me. Fourteen steps to the lift, to the tune of squeaking wheels. Press the call button. Doors swoosh open. Counting down to the ground floor. As I descend, I calculate the bills you got me to pay, making me believe it was my idea. The doors open. 14% of times I make it this far. What I've never done before is cancel every one of the direct debits: rent, phone, gas and electricity. Never called Alice and arranged to stay with her. There's a first for everything.

I can write my own story, can be good with numbers and words. I'm not and never have been either-or. I don't know what this will add up to. Don't know where I'm going, but I'm headed somewhere. Not trapped in flimsy promises of magic carpet rides to Babylon that never amounted to more than a grubby weekend in Brighton. All that's left are the remaining six steps across the lobby and to the outer door. Through the glass, I see the cab pull up. My phone pings: *Your taxi has arrived.* The door release button is winking green for go.

THE NAMES OF STARS

I tell him I'm fetching the decorations. The attic is one of the few places he won't follow. He hates the fold-down ladder, hates spiders even more. I sit in the dust and nurse my jaw. He's always sorry, although never enough to stop.

John and Penny – I still call them *the children*, even if they have children of their own - have been here half an hour, their toddlers in tow. I don't know why they do this to themselves every Christmas, considering how fast it goes downhill: his descent into drunken screaming, his tears, his snivelling self-pity.

He's already raising his voice. One of the grandchildren – Charlotte, I think – squeezes out an experimental wail.

There are fewer decorations to store each year: glass angels stamped underfoot, hurled against a wall. I flip open a box at random and incandescence sends me sprawling backwards.

I'd forgotten about the star. The family clubbed together for his birthday, back when we still believed he could change. *Just think, Dad!* said Penny. *Your name in lights, for real!* The cardboard is ragged with scraps of wrapping paper from where he didn't bother to open it properly before shoving it aside.

"You poor thing," I say.

The star hoists itself on spindly filaments, blinking feebly, and flicks out a small yellow tongue. My knuckles blister. I'm surprised when there's no pain. The gift certificate is still attached to the lid. Singed around the edges, but I can read the name: *Andrew Michael Walford*.

"Well now, Andrew."

It flashes me an irritated look. I rub my eyes until the dazzle fades. No reason why a star should relish a name foisted onto it by carbon-based lifeforms of the sort that spark and extinguish in less than a blink of its eye.

"I'm sorry," I say. "Of course that's not what you're called."

It nods forgiveness. I wonder what its true name is, and how impossible to pronounce.

"Marian!" screams Andrew, from the foot of the ladder. "What in hell are you doing?"

"Mum?" calls John, hopefully. "Dad's ever so sorry. It was a silly mistake."

He always was a fool. He still is, even though he's grown.

The star glances at the skylight, with an encouraging expression. I open the window wide enough for escape, grab hold of the box.

"It won't be dark for a couple of hours."

The star vibrates gently, and I realise it's giggling. A bizarre sensation, holding a happy star in your arms. It *was* a daft thing to say. The stars are always there. It's only us who can't see them in daylight. It clambers out, creaking from its imprisonment. When it turns and looks back, I think it's to say, *thank you*; but this is a long way from gratitude. Downstairs, the thunder of arguing and squalling infants. In a while, there'll be a slammed door, a car gunning its engine.

I reach up, grasp a fiery hand.

"Only five minutes," I gasp. "Then I'll have to get back."

We are past Jupiter before I remember what counts for five minutes in the mind of a star.

ONE DAY I'LL FLY AWAY

After Mum starts complaining, I make a sandwich, climb onto the roof and turn the radio up loud enough to drown her out. All I can get is crackle. I twist the dial until I hit on a clear station: *Smooth Love 109*. Love is the last thing on my mind. After *The Wind Beneath My Wings* and *Love Lifts Us Up,* I've had enough.

"When do I get to have wings?" I moan to the setting sun.

I watch Dad back the car into the driveway. Mum will tell him about me being unreasonable, which I am not. She's unreasonable. I tick off the seconds before all hell breaks loose. The house stays quiet. I shuffle along the roof ridge to the chimney, hear the whoosh of a cork popping, glasses clinking.

Shelter from the Storm comes on the radio. It starts to drizzle. I'll sit here all night if I have to. Sooner or later, Mum will start worrying I'll fall off the roof, or get hit by lightning. The hours grind by, the songs stay schmaltzy. I wait for help, with no idea what help I want, or what it'll look like when it arrives.

Around midnight, the front door pops open and Mum and Dad skip down the garden path, Dad in matador pants and my mother with a rose between her teeth. From where I'm perched, it looks like they're doing the cha-cha-cha.

One after the other, the neighbours open their doors. The street fills with adults acting like they don't care. Dozens of them, blowing squeakers, firing off party poppers, waving to each other, champagne bottles in their fists. Under a streetlight, I spot my parents kissing like lovers in a movie.

"Stop that right now!" I shout. "It's disgusting!"

They're either ignoring me or can't hear. I decide they can't hear. They kick up their heels, forming a conga line that stretches to the corner. I watch them weave out of sight, all of them cheering and laughing as they leave their homes, their lives and their children behind them.

MAMA THE KNIFE

She swings her blade like a pirate cutlass, making the air sing to the dance. We kids have to be careful. Papa says she'll slice our fingers off if she isn't handled right. Only he dares take her into his arms. Better than anyone, he knows the balance of her moods, but still wears bandages around his hands.

We hear the way he gasps when Mama holds him close, whispering words we can't understand. Hear steel grinding against granite. We see the little cuts around his mouth.

Our teachers shake their heads, ask about our home situation. Use words like *child services* and *protection*, say it'd only take one phone call. Say we have the right to be safe. Their expressions are hungry.

I fold my arms and say, "Best Mama in the world."

My sisters and brothers fold their arms and nod. We're a damn sight safer than they are. Mama teaches us the best lessons: how to sharpen up. How to carry yourself through the world and all its fear. How to shine bright, edges keen enough to cut through any crap.

A TRIP TO THE ZOO

"I can't believe you've brought me here," you said, twisting the hair over your right ear. "I hate zoos. The whole caged animal thing."

"Oh, come on," I said. "You wanted to go to a bullfight when we were in Spain last year. The only reason we didn't was you got the wrong day."

"*You* got the wrong day. And it's completely different."

"No, it's not."

You went quiet, in that way that said the conversation was over.

"Because the bulls aren't behind bars?" I said, knowing there was no point.

You stood in front of the sunburnt hoarding which informed us in French, English and Arabic that the big cats were down the path to the left. We passed cage after cramped cage of miserable creatures.

"Not exactly Windsor Safari Park," you muttered.

"So, do you want to leave or don't you?"

You strode ahead, towards the big cat enclosure. The air was tarpapered with the solid reek of tom-cat. The beast was collapsed onto its side; a dappled heap of sandy pebbles drooping under the weight of its spots. The tip of its tail tasted the rise and fall of the air. After a lazy moment, the pile of golden rocks stirred. Its nose was dry and cracked; a scar scribbled across its right cheek. You muttered something.

"What?"

"His stride is wildernesses of freedom."

"Uh?"

"Ted Hughes."

"The man who reads the news?"

You shrugged. "Mmph."

"It's not striding. It's not even moving."

"You wanted to come here. Why don't you poke it with a stick?"

Without standing up, it twisted to face us. It unlocked an eye, looked at me: closed it. Opened both eyes and looked at you: held them open. Its ears twitched: the tongue of its tail continuing to lick away the dusty afternoon.

"Lions only move their tails when they're angry," I said.

"It's a leopard."

"I know. You're always telling me things I know already."

The animal swiped its nose with a vast pink tongue; stretched out a lazy foreleg and raked the dust. It yawned, fogging me with dead breath. The two of you stared at each other.

"Smile," I said, hoisting my new camera.

"Cats can't smile," you sighed.

"I know that too," I sighed back. "Stand this way a bit, then I'll get you both in."

"It's cruel," you said, turning your face away and ruining the shot. "I'm going back to the hotel."

We spent the remainder of the fortnight drinking local beer. You were in bed beside me every time I woke up. We ripped off our all-inclusive hotel bracelets on the bus to the airport, and I dropped the plastic strip onto the floor between my feet. You folded yours carefully and put it in the back pocket of your jeans. I kissed the side of your cheek and you didn't pull away.

"It's always sad, going home," I said. You patted my knee and leaned into my shoulder. "But we have a lot of happy memories, don't we?"

The first night back, I found you at the bedroom window, hands gripping the sill. You stepped sideways, to let me see. The sky was flickering with scarves of pale rust against the darker orange of the Manchester night.

"Good God," I said. "What is it?"

"The Northern Lights. You hardly ever see them this far south. That must be why we're not getting all the colours, just this brown sparkly effect."

"I've got to get my camera."

When I returned, you were leaning out of the window. For one stupid moment, I thought you were climbing out.

"Don't," I said, without meaning to. Your head was so far out you didn't hear me.

I looked over your shoulder. In the garden, next to the bushes, was a leopard, curling itself into a spring: chin down, backside wriggling upwards. Its eyes picked out the glow in the sky and threw two golden coins at us. It shut its eyes: the lamps winked out.

"What was that?" I gasped.

"Nothing," you said, turning away.

"It was a leopard."

"No, it wasn't. This is Manchester."

"It was right there," I said, pointing. The shadows under the rhododendron were empty black ink.

"Where?" you said, peering in the direction of my finger.

"It's gone," I breathed. "Hey, where are you going?"

"I need the toilet."

The next morning I woke to find you standing in front of the wardrobe.

"Why don't you get rid of these clothes?" you said.

"They're almost new. There's nothing wrong with them."

"Wear them, then."

"Ok, ok," I replied, waving my hands.

You went downstairs. I called after you, "How about you make me a coffee?"

"Just the way you like it," you shouted from the kitchen. "I'll be right up."

You came back with a tray, a purple flower off the rhododendron in an eggcup.

"Darling," I said, and kissed you. "It's a lovely day. Why don't we go for a drive? We can be in the Lakes in an hour and a half."

"Not this weekend. I've got too much marking to get done for next week."

"Oh."

I watched you dress, gather up your files from your desk, leave the room. "I thought you were marking?"

"I'm going to take it out into the garden," you called from partway down the stairs. "You're right. It's a lovely day."

I drank my coffee slowly. It was far too soon to be getting up on a Saturday. It was cold by the time I finished it, but still good. You made the best coffee ever. I would tell you.

I picked up the bale of weekend papers you'd brought up while I was still dozing. Business section. On the floor. Jobs and Money. I had both. Floor. Sport. For later. Review. Floor. Colour supplement: you'd want that. Travel. Always the thinnest section, and the only one I ever wanted to read. It was full of smug-eyed families rediscovering gites in the south of France.

I scoured the ads at the back. You deserved better than Tunisia, even if it was four-star with a private beach. I checked out prices for the Maldives and St. Lucia. We could stretch to that by next year. And I would definitely lose weight.

I got out of bed and stood sideways to the mirror, breathed in the slackness of my stomach. All it needed was a hundred sit-ups a night; maybe fifty. I'd tighten up in no time.

I looked out of the window. You had set up a folding table and were sitting with your back to the house. A breeze lifted itself into the heat of the morning and the shadows under the bushes prowled from left to right. You flicked the end of your pen with your thumb, spotted a mistake and pounced, underlining it in red ink.

You went to bed early, a pain in your shoulders.

"It's tingling all the way down to my wrists," you said, and held them out as though you were inviting me to handcuff you.

"Do you want some painkillers?"

You dropped your arms. "Yes. I'll take some and crash out."

"It's not even nine o'clock."

"It *hurts*. Pain is tiring. Darling."

You were a humped rock under the covers when I joined you three hours and a bottle of Chilean red later. I put my hand on your shoulder and you squirmed away with a growl.

"I thought you were awake," I lied.

I lay and listened to the purring of your breath until I fell asleep. Almost straight away it was light again. I'd had no dreams at all, and turned over to tell you how weird that was, but you were already up. You'd left a nest in the duvet where you'd curled and slept.

"Hey, where's my delicious coffee?" I called.

You couldn't hear me and I didn't want to shout. I rolled over and looked at the clock. Nearly eleven in the morning. I got out of bed and my knees buckled, sending me tumbling back onto the mattress.

"Your sore arms must be catching," I said to the empty room.

I made wobbling strides to the top of the stairs, shaking off the pins and needles with each step. I called your name as I went down, and again at the door of the kitchen. My stained wine glass was where I'd left it. The back door was bolted.

"Darling!" I called, keeping my voice warm and playful. My armpits were sticky.

The sunshine was bright against the window, showing it clogged with a veil of dirt, but I still caught a flash of you by the bushes, crouching almost out of sight. I slammed back the bolts and opened the door onto a deserted garden. A gale blew out of the mouth of the sun and I choked on the sudden stink of bonfires and tom-cat.

THE KINGDOM OF THE CATS

Her eyes were of gold, of gold, of gold,
And she was most old, most old.

Listen, my little ones! Gather close, my kittens! I shall tell our secret history: our journey from there to here, from darkness into light, from dreary to delectable. Lucas was the first to hear the call. A simple boy, yet he was the opener of the way. In her hut at the village edge, Old Ana stirred her midnight brew and watched him stumble past, taking footstep after footstep in the wake of a luscious beast. She wore the likeness of a jaguar, with fat and silent tread. Her eyes glimmered like the foil with which we wrap festival sweets; her pelt was amber spotted with chocolate.

In those old times, we were foolish. We thought Lucas enchanted; thought the great cat led him to his destruction. We raised lanterns, cried his name. Shook the trees in case he might fall out, but all we did was fill our hair with leaves, puddle our boots in mud. Ana took us in, warmed us at her hearth and told us the truth at the heart of the mystery. Told us of the kingdom between earth and sky, the harvest-home of all our longing. As children, we'd heard the fables, dismissed them as fantasies glimpsed only in dreams.

Our dreams had been true all along. We wept for the time wasted. Ana dried our tears.

"Come," she said. "Follow, and be free."

Her eyes were of gold, of gold, of gold,
And she was most old, most old.

Ana led us to the threshold between worlds. Told us how to regain the joy we lost when we shouldered the burden of growing up. The night held its breath as she taught us the words of re-enchantment. It started with our fingers. We watched them curl into claws, and unsheathed talons from the velvet scabbard of our paws. We shed our frail and naked skin; clothed ourselves in the luxury of fur that slides on quicksilver bones. We unrolled our tails, pricked clever ears, dropped to all fours and prowled. With the patience of lions and leopards, we oozed through the door.

Her eyes were of gold, of gold, of gold,
And she was most old, most old.

A trickle became a stream, became a torrent as we crossed into our new home. In that one night, we shook off all that made us human and miserable: the chains of hatred, envy, anger, argument, all that tastes untrue. We cast off hierarchies born of inequity and greed; shook off the lose-lose binary of palace or hovel, greed or starvation, worthy or unworthy. Let fools say we surrendered everything. We declare it was a rejoicing to shrug such weight from our shoulders. In the dark, all cats are kin, not king.

Her eyes were of gold, of gold, of gold,
And she was most old, most old.

From the greatest to the smallest, we are feline family: leopard godmothers, ocelot sisters, cougar uncles, tiger brothers, caracal cousins. We miaow, we purr, we hunt, we pounce, we bite. We stretch our jaws and shake the skies with roaring. Most wonderful of all, we yowl gratitude to Ana, to Lucas, and to our jaguar mother who saved us from a broken land, where night was fearsome with starveling shadows. Here, the darkness is delicious. The world we dreamed of but never dared to wish for.

Her eyes were of gold, of gold, of gold,
And she was most old, most old.

Listen, my little ones! Gather close, my kittens! My story is nearly done. When you are grown, I, grandfather Lucas, shall take you to the brink of our kingdom and show you where I first met the jaguar, Mother of All. I shall show you the ruins of what we left behind. A reminder of all we have won, a warning of all we stand to lose.

We shall greet Old Ana, stirring her brew of wondrous herbs, and she will bend and pet us from tip to tail. We shall curl around her ankles and she will remark, *What a pretty thing you are,* and we shall bestow upon her a generosity of purring.

When we murmur, *Come with us,* Ana will smile and shake her head. Someone must watch over the gate. Someone must act the giddy bird when men come with cameras and microphones and machines for detecting disappearance. She knows the truth of what and where we are. Knows about the night of our escape and keeps our secret.

Sleep my little ones. Rest safe, my kittens. Here, the midnight sky is beaten silver, the constellations a river of drizzled cream. See, I am stretching to pluck the sweetest lights from heaven, to make you a supper of stars.

Her eyes were of gold, of gold, of gold,
And she was most old, most old.

EYE FOR AN EYE

I

She hugs the fox fur tight around her throat. It's kept her warm for almost fifty years, but in November has its work cut out. The wind shoves her across North Bridge and down Nicholson Street. A young man scowls at her. She recognises the disapproval, aimed at someone wearing not just the skin of a dead animal, but one with its head and tail on show. She'd like to tell him it has three paws, not four, and that's the only reason Robert could afford it; that it's a fond reminder of a husband long gone. But it's none of his business and besides, she gave up fretting about other people's opinions years ago.

It was also years ago that she discovered her talent for shoplifting. Cameras train their beady eyes everywhere, even on little old ladies, but more often than not they are looking in the wrong direction; much in the same way as the store detectives who trail scruffy women in laddered leggings. She always dresses nicely, even to buy a loaf of bread.

Old-fashioned, she knows, but it reminds her of happy times when people in shops called you by name. She'll settle for politeness. All those kind security guards, returning her wrinkled smile and helping steer her shopping trolley when she aims it at a stacked display of artisanal bread. They never notice how she uses the confusion to slide a can of peas into her coat pocket.

She pauses at the gate of Surgeons' Hall. Something draws her inside. Shelter from the hammering gale would be reason enough, but something more is afoot. Perhaps it's because everything in the museum reminds her how lucky she is. She drifts past cabinet after cabinet of undersized human skeletons with curved spines and legs bent double from rickets. And that phrase, repeated over and over on the display cards: *Died in Childbirth. Died in Childbirth.* Less than a hundred years separates her life from theirs. She blows a kiss to a child-sized woman; a woman she might have been.

The impulse urges her onwards. The only way she can describe it is that she has caught a scent and is compelled to follow. She's in no hurry to return to the ferocious weather, so lets herself be swept up the stairs to the Pathology Gallery. Rank upon rank of shelves stretch to the ceiling, crammed with bones in sweetie jars sealed with ancient black tar. She never knew there were so many lost parts in the city. Her gaze is tugged to a particular bottle on the third shelf. Inside, a skeletal hand spreads like a fan stripped of its lace webs. It curves a finger, beckoning her to approach.

What a foolish notion. She shakes herself, and the fox fur quivers. You'd think she was truly dotty, not simply good at pretending. The bones have been wired and arranged in the gesture, that's all. But her feet will not let her leave the spot. This is where she has been brought.

She examines the label. *Left radius and ulna, metacarpal bones and phalanges. Fracture, gunshot, primary amputation.* Even taking into account how tiny everyone was back then, it strikes her as the hand of a young lad – *yes*, an inner voice whispers, *that's right, a lad.* Drummed into a militia, barely old enough to shoulder a gun, and he gets a bullet in the wrist for his trouble. All at once she can see him, clear as day, held down by his comrades as the field doctor saws his arm off halfway to the elbow. She hears the butcher chide his shrieking victim, *better a bullet to the hand than the ballocks. Now, there's a nasty place to go rotten.* Tutting and shaking his head as he swipes the boning knife in a swift arc. *Hush your caterwauling! I never heard the like from a fellow your age. Away off now to your mammy and get some tar on that stump and you'll be right as rain in no time, so you will.*

The boy waves, forlornly, from his glass prison. She raises her own hand and waves back. Poor lonely soul, she thinks. The display shelves are fronted with narrow strips of Perspex. Wide enough to stop the exhibits falling out, but not wide enough to stop someone slipping their hand within. She glances around, casually: fewer bug-eyed cameras than the supermarket; no uniformed guards stalking the corridors. She wriggles her fingers past the plastic barrier and caresses the lid of the boy's flask. No-one stamps across the parquet floor and ticks her off. The glass canister is very slim. Why, it would fit through the gap.

No. Preposterous. She mustn't even think it. But she does think it, and more. There are no trolleys with which to provide distraction, but she is up to the challenge. She shifts position to shield what she's doing, grasps the jar and edges it through the slot. It's rather like posting a parcel in reverse. With a fluid movement perfected during years of shopping expeditions, she pockets it, fluffing up her fox fur to disguise the gesture. Less time than it takes to draw a breath. She'll be caught, of course, but somehow that's the last thing that matters.

She shuffles the remaining containers together to fill the empty space and trots down the stairs and into the courtyard. Despite the chill, she flops onto a bench to catch her breath. Any moment now, a member of the museum staff will bear down upon her, demanding the return of their specimen. She'll hand it over, complete with her finest impression of a harmless old dear who said it was calling out to her.

It was, but that's not the point.

No-one comes. No-one growls, *come this way, please.*

A few flakes of snow escape from the leaden sky and sting her face. She ought to feel guilty about her terrible theft. It's part of a person, for heaven's sake. There's not a twinge.

When her heart has stopped pattering, she stands up and ambles through the stone archway. Back on Nicholson Street, the wind is sharp enough to cut granite. She rubs her hands to coax some warmth back into them. By a stroke of luck, the bus to Dalkeith pulls up just as she reaches the stop. All the way home, the fox tickles her ear. The rocking of the bus makes it wag its tail, slowly and happily.

She stands the bottle on the kitchen table. The hand has fallen against the glass, what with all the jiggling on the bus. She prises off the lid, releasing a puff of trapped air and the scent of smoke. She wriggles her fingers inside to set it upright and in doing so, shakes hands with the boy. She's surprised by warmth. It is almost furry to the touch. *How ridiculous*, she scolds herself. *What did she put in her tea this morning; whisky?*

She waits for her imagination to iron out its creases, but the bones remain silky. They could be part and parcel of her fur wrap, for goodness' sake. She glances at the fox, stretched flat on the tabletop. Its eyes glint.

"What a pair we make," she says.

The fox smiles. Whoever said animals have no sense of humour never had one about the house.

"Trio," she corrects herself.

She carries the boy's jar into the sitting room and positions him on one end of the mantelpiece. He makes a perfect counterpoint for the urn containing her dear Robert's ashes. No; not a trio. A quartet. Together they make quite the family.

II

I dreamed of him every night. I knew I'd find a way to make it up to him, eventually. He didn't deserve my vengeance. He didn't set that snare; was simply unlucky enough to find it. If only he'd walked away. If only he hadn't kept my paw.

With the eye of memory I see him, clear as if it were yesterday. Sent to check the traps, he finds my severed foot in the iron jaws of the largest. The chewed edge is wet and the drops of blood leading away into the bracken are fat and fresh, and not a single fly has had time to settle upon the meat. He is astonished that I – a dumb animal – bit off my own foreleg rather than let myself be taken.

Not only that, but I must have gnawed through the bone in silence, because he recalls how he's not heard a whimper all morning. He wrestles it free, takes it home and stows it in the chimney until it smells of a fire in the forest. He thinks it'll bring him luck. The poor fool should know that good fortune comes from rabbits, not vixens.

My body cries out for what it lacks and my lost paw answers. Wherever he carries me, I follow, the hunted becoming the hunter. I don't know why I do this, because no-one can return what has been torn away. I pray to the God of Foxes for my paw to be restored. When that is refused, I pray for restitution. For revenge. A lifetime of snapping chicken necks has made me spiteful and stupid. I watch, and wait, and when I have my chance, I seize it.

Like all young men, he is in a hurry to throw his life away for king and country, and that's how he finds himself at the wrong end of more guns than I've ever had to face. But what I desire takes only one bullet. I watch the battle from a safe distance. When my chosen assassin shoulders his gun, I send my trickster spirit to whisper in his ear: *left now, a little more to the left.* I feel the curl of his finger around the trigger.

Oh, the pull.

I watch the bullet fly and pierce the arm of my thief. A paw for a paw. A fair exchange, I think, as I hop away in a pretty 1-2-3, 1-2-3, waggling my pert russet backside in the way that intoxicates many a dog-fox hereabouts. Let him keep my severed part, tucked into my shirt as a talisman. I only want his hand, not his heart.

So it is that I find myself, all these years later, outside the Surgeons' Hall and draped around the throat of a woman not much younger than me. I scent the lad as soon as we pass. Unmistakeable, even now. I nudge her through the electronic door and up the stairs to where his perfume is strongest; the room where all the exiled limbs of men and women are stored. I can still see, though my eyes are glass. Mine is the eye of desire, strong enough to outlive breath.

There it is: his sawn-off hand, marooned in its lonely bottle and set between a gangrenous finger and a shattered knee. It has been stripped of its pretty meat, bones arranged in that gesture used by priests when blessing their flocks. I would raise my remaining paw in salute, but my bones were removed a long time ago. Of course, I'm the one who prompts the old woman to filch the jar. It's no different to dragging a hen through the slats in a coop.

I am comforted. As happens so often, I regretted my act of vengeance as soon as it was committed. I tried to tell myself I was justified, and repeated that lie to my cubs so often I almost grew to believe it. However, I knew it was not the boy's fault, any more than it was mine for stealing his Master's chickens.

It's only since I commenced this second life as a fur wrap that I have learned the softness of forgiveness. I've hugged this woman close, have listened to her fears and frustrations, and realised how similar we are, beast and woman. Let us share this second life.

See; she is opening the lid. She is reaching in. She is shaking his hand.

A MANCHESTER ENCOUNTER, OR,
THE BLACK DOG OF PETERLOO

From an unpublished and anonymous letter now in the collection of the Portico Library, Manchester. Typography dates it to the first quarter of the nineteenth century. Spelling and punctuation have been adapted for ease of the modern reader.

"How often do we pass through life recalling chance encounters of the briefest duration? Against all reason, we remember a snatched conversation or a face glimpsed in a crowd, rather than those interactions born of long and amiable acquaintance.

There is no man living who does not recall the calamitous events of the 16th of August just passed. It was then I saw him, on Saint Peter's Fields, amongst our band of comrades crying out for enfranchisement. He was a fellow of swarthy mien, dense of whisker and grim of visage; yet for all that he was my brother and I would have called him such. I had not met him previously: not at any meeting; nor in any one of the multitude of low public houses frequented by men of his sort – or of the sort I took him for; nor did I clap eyes on him afterwards. Yet our meeting, which was no meeting, has remained in my mind with great clarity.

He moved through the company, glancing from side to side as though searching for some person. His gait was unbalanced, as though there was a great pain in his ankles, most dolorous to bear. The shoulders of his jacket were gnawed at the seam and the fabric of his shirt peeped through. I remarked privately upon the whiteness of that shirt, which, set against the slovenliness of his garments otherwise, seemed to my eye most remarkable.

More notable still was the matter of his hair. He was a hairy man: more hirsute than Esau and the most thickly-pelted fellow I ever met. His nose, what I could see of it, was prominent and surrounded by a dense undergrowth of beard and moustaches. I wondered if he encouraged such a riot of facial hair in an attempt to disguise the vast size of his snout. If he did, it was not a successful stratagem. The tip glistened with unwiped moisture and besides, his lips were so thin as to give his mouth the appearance of a wide rent in a fur muffler, with teeth glinting through the gash.

Then there was the manner in which he tugged the brim of his hat over his left eye, as though he craved to shield that half of his face men dub the *sinister*. I imagined he bore some disfiguring mark and had wearied of gawping stares. My heart surged with fellow-feeling, for I too bear a disfigurement, albeit not of the visible sort. Perhaps it was that drew me after him, as surely as a child follows a piper.

Making one's way through a press of bodies is never a simple task, but this man slid through the congregation as easily as a knife through warmed butter, and I trotted in his wake with greased facility. There followed the most singular of occurrences. He paused, one foot raised and one touching the earth, snuffed the air with his long nose, reached into the wall of bodies, and brushed a woman on the shoulder. At first, I thought he greeted a friend, but when she turned I knew from her demeanour it was not so. I have seen paler faces only on the freshly-deceased, when all blood drains away into the nether limbs. This was not terror however; not at all – rather some emotion far more profound. I watched her features shift from questioning, to refusal, to denial and finally settle upon calm acceptance; and all of this in the time it would take to tear a piece of bread in half. Then and only then, he withdrew his hand and it resumed its habitual position, gripping the hat-brim in order to cast his face in shadow.

I could not stir. All forward motion was arrested as surely as if my knees were made of gravy. The crowd tossed me to and fro and I believe I would have toppled at the insistence of their jostling, if the hairy man had not glanced in my direction and grinned. I wish I had turned tail and run, for it would have been the wiser course of action. Do not think me brave, however. I was as craven as a cur that is hauled on a chain by its master. Fifteen more times I watched as he paused, reached out his paw and laid it upon the shoulder of some unsuspecting soul. Fifteen times I saw the same change of expression, the same eldritch peace at the close. Man, woman, child: he spared no-one.

I wondered why he did not touch me. Here I was, a faithful disciple and upon me he bestowed nothing. I dashed to his side and clapped my hand upon his shoulder, which heaved, with weeping or laughter I had no notion. He twisted his neck, further than I thought possible for a man to do without snapping his spine, and glanced at me slantwise. It was only at this close proximity that I noticed the smell of him: the reek of pork left on a windowsill so long even a dog will not purloin it. He bared those long teeth I had hitherto only glimpsed, and shook his head, the lank rats' tails of his hair swinging in time.

"Ask not, and be fortunate," he barked.

I opened my mouth, for I seethed with needy questions. Before I could spill one of them, he laughed; a huffing sound halfway between a wheeze and a strangle. Then he turned and bounded through the mob. As he sped away, his coat tails flapped and I saw, between them, bushy as the brush of a fox, his tail."

A SHIFT IN TIME ZONES

At breakfast, she lays Harold's place: toast the way he likes it, just turning brown; a jar of thick-cut marmalade. She doesn't like how the rind gets stuck in her dentures, but it's his favourite.

Her son, Ben, knocks on the window and waggles his hand. He's in and out at all hours, *keeping an eye on her* as he puts it. That's all very well, but sometimes she wishes he would give her a bit of peace, especially this time of the morning. He lets himself in, sits at the head of the table and helps himself to tea. When he reaches for the toast, she glares until he withdraws his hand.

"I thought it was for me."

"You're sitting in Harold's chair," she says.

He rolls his eyes. "You're not still setting two places, are you?" he says, through a slurp.

"What's wrong with that?"

He puts down the cup, slowly and carefully. "Mum," he says, in the voice you use when a six-year-old is taking far too long to understand the two-times table. "It's been weeks. You have got to move on."

She knows Ben means well, but he's like the rest of the family, every last one of them telling her it's *high time she stopped living in the past*, and to reset her watch to the present. But this is nothing like adjusting the clocks forward in spring or back in the autumn. She wants to keep her life set to the time zone she lived in only a month and a half ago, when Harold was still alive.

Ben grabs a piece of toast before she can slap the back of his hand and starts on another of his favourite subjects: lecturing her how she should turn the garage into a granny flat, how the house is too big for her to manage, and wouldn't she be happier if she sold it and went into a—.

She stops listening when he gets to that point. She *is* home. She was carried over the threshold in Harold's arms, and when her time comes, she'll be carried out. There is no other place – or time – she wants to be. She has no desire to live in Ben's world, where all he does is fuss about needing a new car or a new sofa, when there's nothing wrong with the ones he has.

No point in arguing. There's a glitter in his eye whenever he steers the conversation to money, and she doesn't want to think badly of him. She considers telling him to mind his own business, in language that would make his toes curl. Working as a nurse all those years, she picked up fruity language that could turn the air blue as a pair of sailor's trousers. Ben can take his unwanted advice and—.

She takes a patient breath and looks out of the window. She wishes Ben wouldn't treat her as though she's off with the fairies, putting bacon in the teapot and her slippers in the oven. She may be 82, but there's nothing wrong with her mind.

Besides, living in the past is a matter of opinion. A scientist on the television said that time is happening all at once, so there's no such thing as past or present. Not that she needs scientists to back her up. Life has taught her there's more than one way to look at time, and how to pass through it. Like the holiday in New York, when she and Harold couldn't figure out the clocks; so they got up at 4am and went to bed at 7pm. So what if they were out of rhythm with everyone else? They still got to ride the ferry and see Lady Liberty, with Harold singing *The Bronx is up and the Battery's down* in his lovely baritone.

She sighs. In the garden, moles are stirring the earth into soft puddings. The longer she looks, the more she's convinced they're dotted across the grass in a deliberate arrangement. Ben stops pontificating and follows the line of her gaze.

"You should get rid of those moles. They're ruining a perfectly good lawn."

"Yes, dear," she says, trying to work out what the pattern reminds her of.

One of the moles sticks its head out of a fresh heap and waves a paw. She waves back. She could swear they're building the constellation of Orion in mud pies. Harold will be tickled pink.

"Mum!" shouts Ben, his face going that funny colour it does when she ignores him.

He'll storm out shortly. Then she'll be able to get back to what she was doing, out of step with everyone else. When she hears the front door slam, she shuffles to the kitchen, makes a fresh pot of tea and slides two slices of bread into the toaster. The smell drifts up the stairs. In their bedroom, Harold will be catching a whiff of it.

"Come and see what the moles are up to," she calls, gently.

He is sliding his tired old feet into his slippers. He moves a lot slower these days. Any minute now, he'll be at her side.

FACTS OF MATTER

She swerves off the road, gunning the engine. Rear-view mirror a spray of pebbles and loose earth. Wheels spin and gears complain as she screeches up the hill towards the trees. She grinds to a halt; wrenches the door open. It swings like a broken arm.

Steep slog upwards. From the road, the dividing line between forest and not-forest looked clear. Now she's leaving one and entering the other, it's far less obvious. She concentrates on walking: right foot lift and swing; heel down and push. Left foot lift and swing. Repeat. Repeat. There was a time she climbed hills without thinking.

Finally, she can't see the way back. Around her ankles, saplings tug the hem of her skirt with small sharp fingers. Leaves rustle with a comforting shush. Her heartbeat slows. She will not remember the mess, the way some things can't be repaired; the way promises and people can be broken so easily.

A river of fallen pine needles slides her forwards. She falls into step with the broken rhythm of dripping, a code tapped out by water. All she need do is follow its encouragement. The forest exhales, breath swaying the branches. A slow and gracious beckoning.

Who better to trust than trees, who watch us flare, gutter and wink out in the time it takes to grow a branch? She's done with the effort of being human: its shrill insistence on superiority, the universe a toy created for amusement and exploitation. Holding out an arm, she waits.

From wrist to elbow, each faint hair pricks upright. Scent of warm resin. Skin crackles, stiffens into bark; fingers unfold twigs. Toes pierce the soil and dig into earth's wet heart. Roots twine up her calves and hold her steady. Bruises unpeel, shed yellow leaves. Breath quits her lungs, the splinters of her heart unpluck and scatter. Hair swirls, feathering upwards as heat she no longer needs ripples from her flesh. The forest gathers her into its arms.

This is not diminishing. This is not surrender. It is a shift of perspective. Not one particle of her being has been lost, simply reconfigured. She is far from the body's frantic complication of blood, bone, certainty; the imperative of belonging. There is a split in the sky, growing wider. She soars towards it, fluttering in the space between the trees.

HAPPY EVER AFTER WITH BEAR

The road trip is going long. We steer clear of the phrase *running away* in case it breaks the spell. I know about spells. My father read a bedtime story where the prince was a bear until someone said, *Hey, you're a bear* and crack, the magic broke apart and he was back in his ordinary body and it was supposed to be a perfect ending.

You shift gear and machinery grinds. If not for you and this car, I'd be stuck in a hungry life that had chewed me to the bone. I knew we had a chance when I said, *I don't sleep nights* and you said, *OK.* Not, *Why?* or, *That's stupid*, or, *You can do anything if you want to badly enough.*

The car stinks, an animal odour that blooms in the evening, and though we've never managed to pin down where it's coming from, I'm guessing it's me. I love the rankness; everything a journey should be, away from that and towards this.

I drag a blanket from the back, choked with dog hair. My father said we had hairy hearts, me and him, which was what made us warm. I wondered what my mother's was made of. She won the custody case, not because she loved me, but because she hated him.

"Grr," I say.

"Woof," you reply, gunning the engine.

The headlights sweep a stand of trees and I see faces looming out of the bark and because we promised no secrets, I tell you. You peer into the shadows and say, "It's ok, they're good trees. Friendly faces."

We crest the hill and break free from the tree line. My heart is quaking like a newborn lamb. I'm in awe of the way they stagger upright within minutes of being born, racing around a moment after. In that fairy tale where the prince was a bear, he had a stag inside him. Inside the stag was a wolf, and inside the wolf was a fox, and inside the fox was a lamb, heart skittering. I've never minded the leaping inside my chest.

Sun's coming up. You ruffle the hair cropped over my ears, the stubble trying my chin for size. You believe in me, whatever shape I'm in. Never once have you said, *Hey, you're a bear* and broken the spell. Never once asked, *Are you feeling more human?* as though that's all there is to aim for.

It's time for me to take the wheel. To look out of the window and think about how love is holding back on questions we can't answer. Love is the drive, the car, the road, unrolling.

ACKNOWLEDGEMENTS

Some of these stories have been placed in competitions, or first appeared in the following journals and anthologies.

Amphibian, Bath Flash Fiction Award, BBC The Verb, BBC Write on Tyne, Bear Creek Gazette, Best British Short Stories 2024, Black Dog Tales, Bolton Review, Books Ireland Flash, The Bristol Short Story Prize, The Cabinet of Heed, Casket of Fictional Delights, City Secrets, Confingo, Darkest Midnight in December, Dark in the Day, Disturbing the Beast, Fictive Dream, FlashFlood, Flash 500, The Interpreters House, Janus Literary Journal, Largehearted Boy, Litro, Longleaf Review, Lost Balloon, Lunate, Manchester Review, Miramichi Flash, National Flash Fiction Day, New Flash Fiction Review, Paper Crow, Practise to Deceive, Retreat West, Seaside Gothic, Spot on Stories, The Art of Tying Knots, The Forgotten and the Fantastical, Under the Radar, Wigleaf 50 longlist, Wolf Girls.

About the Author

Rosie Garland writes short and long fiction, poetry and hybrid works that fall between and outside definition. She's lead singer in post-punk band The March Violets. Poetry collection 'What Girls Do In The Dark' (Nine Arches Press) was shortlisted for the Polari Prize 2021; her novel The Night Brother was described by The Times as *"a delight...with shades of Angela Carter."* Val McDermid has named her one of the most compelling LGBT+ writers in the UK today. Her latest novel, 'The Fates' (Quercus) is a retelling of the Greek myth of the Fates. In 2023 she was made Fellow of the Royal Society of Literature.

About Fly on the Wall Press

A publisher with a conscience.
Political, Sustainable, Ethical.
Publishing politically-engaged, international fiction, poetry and cross-genre anthologies on pressing issues. Founded in 2018 by founding editor, Isabelle Kenyon.

Some other publications:

The Soul We Share by Ricky Ray

The Unpicking by Donna Moore

Lying Perfectly Still by Laura Fish

Modern Gothic - Anthology

And I Will Make of You a Vowel Sound by Morag Anderson

The Dark Within Them by Isabelle Kenyon

Secrets of the Dictator's Wife by Katrina Dybzynska

The Process of Poetry Edited by Rosanna McGlone

Snapshots of the Apocalypse by Katy Wimhurst

Demos Rising Edited by Isabelle Kenyon

Exposition Ladies by Helen Bowie

The Truth Has Arms and Legs by Alice Fowler

Climacteric by Jo Bratten

The State of Us by Charlie Hill

The Sleepless by Liam Bell

Social Media:

@fly_press (X)

@flyonthewallpress (Instagram and Tiktok)

@flyonthewallpress (Facebook)

www.flyonthewallpress.co.uk